Pusakis at Paros

By the same author

Drama

Fancy Footwork; Labels; Dusty Bluebells; Shyllag;
Dreamkeeper; A Flight of Angels; Kalahari Blues;
Carolan's Cap; Nocturne; Bohemians; Witch Hayzel
of Muddling Manor; The Mighty Oak of Riverwood; A
Wasteland Harvest; Nasturtiums & Cherry Buns;
Easter Eggs; Omlettes; Lemon Soufflé; Dying to be
Young; Chance & the Elixir; The Ring of Mont de
Balison; The Sealwoman & the Fisher;
The Nude who Painted Back (in collaboration with
Mia Gallagher & Nathalie Rafal)
Midhir & the Firefly; The Gold of Tradaree.

Film

Gypsies; Girls in Silk Kimonos; Kevin;
Letter to Ehkaterina; Desire

Radio

Wallace; Shyllag; Carolan's Cap

Fiction

Song for Salamander (2004, Trafford)
Short Stories in anthologies of Irish writing
and international literary journals.

Non Fiction

Let's Help Our Children Talk (O'Brien Press)
Essays in film, educational & arts journals.

Pusakis at Paros

and other stories

Miriam Gallagher

Acknowledgements
Grateful thanks to the editors of these anthologies & literary journals, in which several of
the stories, or versions of them, originally appeared: *Arabesques Press; A Page Falls Open;
New Grapevine; The Turning Tide; WP Journal; Wilderness House Literary Review.*

Cover Design by: Gerhardt Gallagher

Note for Librarians: A cataloguing record for this book is available from Library
and Archives Canada at www.collectionscanada.ca/amicus/index-e.html

Printed in Victoria, BC, Canada.

ISBN: 978-1-4251-4977-2

www.trafford.com

North America & international
toll-free: 1 888 232 4444 (USA & Canada)
phone: 250 383 6864 ♦ fax: 250 383 6804
email: info@trafford.com

The United Kingdom & Europe
phone: +44 (0)1865 722 113 ♦ local rate: 0845 230 9601
facsimile: +44 (0)1865 722 868 ♦ email: info.uk@trafford.com

10 9 8 7 6 5 4 3 2

Contents

About the Author

Miriam Gallagher, Irish playwright, novelist & screenwriter, has studied Drama in London (LAMDA). Her work, staged & screened in Ireland, London, Paris, USA & Canada, is included in the *Field Day Anthology of Irish Writing* and profiled in *Irish Women Writers: An A-Z Guide* (Greenwood Press, CT, USA, 2006). Her work is translated into several languages.

She has published a novel, *Song for Salamander*, (Trafford 2004) and Short Stories in anthologies of Irish Writing and internationally. *Fancy Footwork* (1997, Soc. Irish Playwrights, 2nd Ed), a book of thirteen produced plays, includes *Fancy Footwork*, *Shyllag* and *The Ring of Mont de Balison*. A second book of three plays, *Kalahari Blues and Other Plays* was published in 2006 (Mirage, Dublin) Rté has broadcast her radio plays, and her film *Gypsies*, screened in New York's Lincoln Center & San Francisco Plaza Cinemas. Non fiction includes *Let's Help Our Children Talk* (O'Brien Press 1977) and commissioned essays for international literary, film, theatre, educational & arts, journals.

Miriam has received Arts Council & European Script Fund Awards for her feature length screenplay *Girls in Silk Kimonos* (celebrating the Gore Booth sisters) MHA (Mental Health Assoc) Tv Script Award & an EU Theatre Award.

Other awards include a Writer's Exchange to Finland and in 2006, her play, *The Parting Glass*, was an international prizewinner. (USA)

She has worked in professional, prison & community theatre. Commissions include *The Ring of Mont de Balison*, (Ranelagh Millennium Project) *Kalahari Blues* (Galloglass Theatre Co nationwide tour) *The Gold of Tradaree* (Clare Arts Award) *The Mighty Oak of Riverwood* (Betty Ann Norton Theatre School 40 years celebration) performed at the Gate Theatre; and *Fancy Footwork* (Dublin Theatre Festival), performed at the Focus Theatre by Mountjoy prisoners.

She presented work at Semaine Mondiale des Auteurs Vivants de Théâtre and 4th & 5th Int. Women Playwrights' Conferences. She has served as council member of the Society of Irish Playwrights, vice president of Irish PEN, on the Irish Writers Union committee, as a judge for O.Z. Whitehead Play Competition and on the awards panel of Arts & Disability Forum. She has given scriptwriting courses at Rté Training Unit, schools, colleges, prisons and arts centres. She has been a guest lecturer at universities in Ireland, Athens, New York, Boston & Pretoria.

Her mss are in the National Library and film work in the Irish Film Archive.

Web of the
Thespian Giant

The pub was a seedy affair on the seafront - cracked cane furniture and limp curtains flapping at clandestine assignations.

'The usual?'

Putting her wet scarf on the table, she nodded.

As he moved, part of the web floated with him. Only the faint wispy edges remained. She tasted its wispiness and shivered. The smoky ceiling was festooned with dusty fishing nets, heavy with green glass balls. She imagined them being fashioned at dark of night in the glass bottle factory near the docks. She saw them wet and glistening from sweat and furnace, destined for deep green Donegal waters and silver iridescence of mackerel. But instead here they were, choking on waves of stale air to a background of idle chatter. Now he was back putting their drinks on the table, and the web was whole again.

'It won't be long now.'

'Tuesday.'

While he poured the stout, tilting the glass with nonchalant expertise, as on that first time, she watched the thespian giant silently slipping whiskey and stout into his massive frame, as if engaged in some private ritual with mellow yellow and rich cream of comfort. She had decided then not to make a habit of going to the pub after rehearsals but the drink eased some of the awkwardness between them, helping to make an intimate occasion out of their coming together. And it made her talk.

'Here's to us.' He smiled. She raised her glass.

'When will you take your holidays?'

As a child she used to go on holidays to her Granny in Roscommon. There was a rain barrel in the yard - often so full that the sweet soft water spilled over the side. Nothing like it for the hair, her Granny said.

'Holidays! Hmm.' A deprecating sniff as huge hands waved away the very idea. 'Who needs holidays?'

Oh yes, his life a perpetual roundelay of evenings spent with Hecuba - honeywhiskeydew and gallons of stout - nectar that coarsened leonine features and only muffled hungers.

'I get terribly nervous.'

He took her hand in his. 'I know.'

She let her hand rest in the quietness. It was moments like this that made her wonder at the web's silky strength clinging with the lightness of gossamer.

She had first sensed it that night as she left the pub, the giant a towering warmth at her back.

'You read well.'

'Thank you.'

'I look forward to working with you.'

She felt the web stirring in the air between them. It held them together for a dark moment. She broke first.

'I must go. My husband will be wondering what's keeping me.'

Confused and elated, she'd walked to the car for the long ascent to Dalkey and hot cocoa.

Sitting here with the whiskey warming her, she remembered her life before she joined the Patrician Players in search of new horizons. How remote now, almost unreal, seemed her convenient home where sleek machines purred daily, alternating with the evening hum of bridge parties. There once was a time she'd welcomed the secret corners of that cool box of predictability. It was easy to hide, pressing down her individuality with the laundry, letting her energies whirr away in an endless spiral of wash – rinse - spin. Hypnotised by her gleaming Formica shrine and lulled by its chanting she had felt inviolate.

She thought of how the giant had nudged his way into her heart regardless of the fact that there was no room for him. The heavy door of the musty basement where they rehearsed shut the lid firmly on her outside life as she was drawn in deftly by the web's tracery - silvery to the touch and oh so sweet!

Throughout the flurry of rehearsals she could feel the web's power stretching to unite them - filmy strands becoming strong and seductive as silk. She became aware of a contradiction in his eyes - eyes that seemed to say, 'Look at me and exult! Behold my stature is as lionlike as my head and heart!' - while roots of sadness pushed through, beckoning her to yield and let the web live. Yet, to stay alive it needed to be fed by the strength of the living. A lacy visitor turned parasite.

In a dream she tried to break through the thick milky skin that was all around her only to spin round and round in an airy space that was part of the web. It was as if all the airy spaces of the web were waiting for her, silky fingers leaving her breathless from the force of their hold. Then she knew she must yield or break the strands. But, by some mysterious osmosis, the web and her life were becoming absorbed into each other so that she couldn't tell them apart. Like those once luminous green glass balls she was trapped by the dusty net of circumstances.

He lit a cigarette. All the vices - gambling too. One day she'd telephoned only to hear he was watching a race on tv, his horse was fifth, and could she ring back. That was when she meant to tell him but couldn't bring herself to say the actual words. Instead her stainless kitchen mocked with its sterile purity, and she felt accused by the purr of her acrylic temple. Throbbing machines pounded in her head until the sound became a scream that tore at her. She had transgressed by shifting her allegiance and must atone. The smooth machines were screaming for sacrifice.

'You know, I've met you a few years too soon.'

His voice was matter of fact.

She drained her glass. 'I must go.'

'Ah, hold on, it's nearly the Holy Hour. Have another and after that we'll be thrown out.'

'No, I really must go.'

'I'm afraid I'm callous where people are concerned. I have to be free to come and go.'

'You're a cunning operator all right.'

Now was her moment. All she needed to do was tell him simply – no need to elaborate - then the rest would be up to him.

'There's something I've been meaning to say -' she began but stopped when she saw the look of defence in his eyes.

'I must be off.' She rose.

'I'll come with you.'

He finished the remains of his drink and they left together. Outside they stood in the doorway for another of their awkward partings.

'Well, sin é, 'she said.

'Let me know how Tuesday goes.'

'All right.'

'Look, it's clearing up.'

Even as he spoke the web thinned and started to float away from them, moving as if set free.

'Bye so.'

With a wave the giant left her looking at shreds of gossamer - all that remained now of the web - gliding gracefully out towards the horizon to hang like a low mist over the sea. She watched the web's last traces becoming no more than a wisp. A drop of water fell from the lintel onto her face. Gently she brushed it away. Then, turning homewards, she saw that the sky held the promise of fresh rain for the country's rain barrels.

The New Romance

'Have one, dear,' urged Sybil. 'They're from the garden.'

I hesitated. The small green pears, nestling in the basket, looked so perfect. However, she would be offended if I refused. Using my fruit knife with its mother of pearl handle, I cut one lengthways - a neat, almost surgical incision through the centre - and inspected the pale flesh, rimmed with light green, in the centre of each half a pinkish tinge, very faint. The fruit looked so flawless it seemed a shame to eat it. I said so.

'Oh nonsense!' Sybil laughed her tinkly laugh, and waved away my scruples with a jingle of bracelets. 'If you leave them untouched for too long they go off.'

Like us? I wondered, picturing the pair of us decaying from neglect.

'That's the pear tree.' Sybil pointed a manicured finger towards the garden. 'I've had such fun, dear, learning all the names. This one's, *Conference*. A new taste.'

I looked out at the jungle that was Sybil's garden; Loganberries, several gooseberry bushes; a glorious profusion of giant broccoli stubbornly dominating the central area; an espalier pear tree trailing against a wall of super lap.

'I had to erect it, dear. Imagine, one day I looked out and saw two heads peering over the wall. Almost as if they'd been cut off!' Sybil's hand flashed under her chin, conjuring up instant decapitation. 'I couldn't have them popping up all over the place could I?'

If we hadn't met at the hospital like we did it's unlikely that we'd ever have become friends. Yet, in our mutual need we struck up a relationship of sorts, taking turns to meet in each other's houses. And it helped pass the time. Not that time was something we should be trying to kill. I preferred when it was Sybil's turn. Her house - a mews built to Queen Anne specifications - was what we laughingly referred to as a *bijou residence*. I loved the bow windows, warm sunny floors of maple, admired her prints and figurines. I even fancied the brass lamp with a map of India for a shade. Maybe she'd leave that to me if she went first.

'Now dear, I have something to tell you.' Sybil laughed. 'But first I must hear all about Japan.'

She poured clear, sparkling wine from Alsace into our Bristol cut glasses. Special glasses. Everything Sybil had was special, like the small octagonal shaped cups and saucers on the polished wood table.

'Of course, I don't much care for the Japanese.' Sybil cut her pear into neat pieces. 'The war you know. All that cruelty.'

'I went to a conference,' I began.

'Aha! I thought it might be something like that. Have some more wine.'

I longed to share the magic of my Japan. I wanted her to drink it all in; the serenity of Zen gardens in Kyoto; evening mist rising from the fold of the Amagi Mountains; that feeling of beauty and isolation flying over the North Pole. I would never forget gazing from my JAL plane· at the tracery of ice on water; straggles of indigo in the Polar sky; melting ice floes, like a lacy patchwork quilt protecting the roof of the world.

'We crossed the North Pole,' I murmured.

'Really?' Sybil smiled, as she reached for a plate.' Have a Danish cookie. They're delicious.'

I took one and bit into its sugar crusted top.

'It was out of this world flying into the sun. No darkness at all.'

'But you slept surely?'

Sybil's tone had an edge of irritation to it. I shook my head.

'Not a wink?' she asked suspiciously.

'No.'

'You poor dear, how awful! '

'No, I loved it. But then I've always been fascinated by the Arctic.'

'My! You are unusual,' she declared and paused. 'I mean for a woman.'

Sybil was quiet, her braceleted wrists lying slack on the table, the pear uneaten on the little octagonal plate with its marigold rim.

'You see,' I continued, the words tumbling out despite myself. 'I'm attracted to Wally Herbert.'

Sybil's eyebrows rose as she fingered her pearl necklace.

'Really? Who's he? One of your men?'

'An explorer.'

'Oh him! Come along, dear, you must finish these.'

'I couldn't Sybil. Honestly I'd burst.'

'Well if you won't I will. No point in keeping them. I don't believe in hoarding.'

As Sybil ate alternate pieces of pear and biscuit, I pictured Wally Herbert lying in the snow within inches of death while an icy lace almost smothered him. Would I have dared touch that filigree mask, creeping over his bearded face? The very idea made me shiver with fear and daring.

I said quickly, 'I thought the North Pole would be like the top of a Christmas cake, all squashed and snowy.'

'And wasn't it?' she asked, adding as she polished off the last of her pear, 'I'm not so sure about the flavour.'

'It's . . . delicate,' I said.

'Mmm,' she replied, as if considering a weighty matter.

Dying to spend a penny, I made a move towards the downstairs bathroom with the Portuguese tiles. Sybil stopped me with, 'Don't use that loo! It's Sam's.'

Sam was her dog, a floppy brute, prone to obscure diseases that required the services of a Top Man at the Veterinary College. In gratitude Sybil plied him with decanters of rare whiskey. It'd be cheaper to pay, but Sybil rejoiced in the glory of Sam receiving treatment from a Top Man. I wondered if Sam's vet was like the other men in Sybil's life; Captain Bondi, for instance, with his Hawker Sidley connections and nose for paintings. His exploits usually peppered our conversation.

'When we got back from Venice he'd take me round Bond St. and show me beautiful things,' she once confided.' Of course he didn't bring me to Hawker Sidley's. He lived in the country. A lovely wife. I met her.'

'Ah,' I murmured.

'My sister in Sligo could never understand those postcards from all over the world, saying, *I miss you.*' Her laugh was almost a giggle.

When I returned from the loo Sybil was making tea. She refused my offer of help. 'Thank you, dear, but I'm used to managing alone. One has to these days.' She shuddered. 'Even if you do get someone in, they break things.'

She poured strong brown tea. In my cup a silver spoon stood upright like a soldier.

'Excuse me putting the spoons in first. These cups are 1939. Nothing like that now. I've given up milk. Sugar?'

'No thanks.'

I sipped the tea. It was too strong and tasted of tannin. A far cry from little bowls of Japanese green tea, delicately flavoured.

'Didn't you feel like a giant with all those tiny people?' Sybil asked. 'And for goodness sake what could you actually say to them anyway?'

'The conference took up most of the time.'

'Any interesting men?'

'No. They were all scientists.'

'Ah! Must have been boring then was it?'

'A nice man at the theatre took me into his box.'

'What age? Just you and he alone in the box?'

'It's not like here Sybil. All the boxes are open with little railings. No chairs. You just loll on cushions. Like Romans.'

'It'd be safer on chairs,' she laughed.

'But it's a real social occasion. You bring your lunch. It goes on for hours.'

'Don't tell them here,' she warned. 'They wouldn't know about the railings.'

I ate some pear. The flavour wasn't very strong.

'What do you think of it?' asked Sybil as she munched. 'Because I'm pushing on I can't taste things anymore. But I still have a good appetite.'

'Delicious,' I said.

'Do they have pears like that over there?'

'Not really.'

'That's a pity,' she sighed, looking out at the pear tree. 'I'd like to taste the flavour of a foreign conference.'

As we laughed, I noticed how her eyes glinted. I wanted to ask about her news, but we'd learned at the hospital that timing is everything.

'I thought about you often while I was in Japan. You know, Sybil, there's an air of the Orient about you.'

'Me?' She poured the last of the wine. 'I always thought I was large and noisy.'

'Maybe it's all . . .' I looked through the archway at the collection of figurines, the brass lamp with a map of India for a shade.

'Oh!' she cried, ' You mean all my things. Come and see my new man.'

I followed her across the polished wooden floor to the fireplace. A special fireplace that fitted in perfectly since part of it had been chopped off by a man she'd discovered with a place in an alleyway near Dame St. Anyone else would have made a shambles of it, but Sybil had pulled it off.

'Yes,' I agreed. 'All your things, and the way you keep shuffling about in slippers.'

'You mean my après-ski?' She glanced down at her knitted socks with leather soles. We both laughed.

'Is this your new man?'

I picked up a pale blue porcelain figure. A wise man. With his wispy beard and hooded eyes he looked as if he knew all the answers.

'He's beautiful,' I murmured.

'Of course,' she said quickly, as if to dispel any possible misunderstanding, ' he's Chinese.'

I replaced the figure on the mantelpiece.

'I must show you my pictures of Indochina. You wouldn't believe how beautiful Ankhor is. Indescribable, dear!' She went to a writing desk near the window and opened the lid. 'They should be in here.' She rummaged inside. 'What a place! They looked after you so nicely. Always pressing your nightdress. The French influence you know. Lovely food. And such cleanliness.'

'Well, Japan is absolutely spotless,' I shot back.

'You know,' she exclaimed, searching for the photographs, 'it's the very same in Spain. You just open the doors and sweep out the dust. What am I looking for?'

'Ankhor, not *The Financial Times*,' I replied, noticing a pile of pink newspapers, neatly folded inside the desk.

Sybil laughed. 'I always keep *The Financial Times*. Marvellous for Sam to lie on. And, they make exquisite bin liners.' She handed me a photograph album. 'Let me give you more tea while you look at these.' I opened the album. 'You couldn't imagine,' she was enthusing, 'what it was like with the moon slowly rising over the turrets,

17

or whatever you call them, and Donald - That's my friend from the Foreign Office - and myself - alone in that special place.'

As I looked at the pictures of Ankhor, I realised that trying to make Sybil understand about my Japan was asking too much - like asking for the moon - the very moon she was now describing in Indochina.

'Imagine our surprise when there was a rustle in the shadows.' Her pale blue eyes stared for a moment. 'And, in terror for our lives, we clung to each other.'

'You and Donald?'

'Yes. And who was it but a guide, a relic of the pre-war Tourist Trade. A Japanese actually.' She drank her tea. 'More?'

'I'm fine Sybil, thanks.'

'You're looking frightfully well, dear. Are you plotting any more foreign conferences?'

'I'd love to go back to Japan.'

'But wouldn't that spoil it? '

'Perhaps.' I smiled at her. 'But I may not get another chance.'

We were both silent, not wanting to state the obvious.

'Never mind,' continued Sybil. 'Anyway, you must have felt gigantic with all those small people.' She peered at me. 'Did you get a chance to mingle?'

'We were at the conference mostly,' I replied.

'Except when you were cooped up for hours in the theatre box with that little Japanese man,' she added mischievously.

'But you can't imagine how polite they are.'

'That's because they're overpopulated.'

I toyed with my cup of tea.

'I am enjoying our chat,' she announced. 'Now, just look at this book about Peking.'

She handed me a bundle, wrapped in tissue paper. Inside was a rare book, published in 1916. I turned the pages.

'Fascinating isn't it?'

'Yes it's -'

'You'll wonder why I never mentioned Peking before. Honestly dear, I didn't feel you were ready for it.'

'That was a lovely meal Sybil.'

'All this talk of abroad makes me feel I've been away instead of stuck in this damp city.'

I rose.

'Oh must you go?'

'Afraid so. I've enjoyed it. The fruit was delicious. Thanks for - '

'I do love our chats,' broke in Sybil with a laugh, 'It's such a relief to find someone with whom you can communicate. I mean we're on the same wavelength. The way we see things. I mean I couldn't tell everyone what I'm telling you. People would think I was mad.'

I walked towards the door.

'Before you go,' declared Sybil, 'you must see my new man.'

I glanced towards the mantelpiece.

'But I thought –' My voice trailed off.

'Oh you mean my Chinese!' Sybil's laugh tinkled gaily. 'Really, dear!'

· She produced a photo from the writing desk and with a flourish swept it before my gaze. A young man with blond hair, wearing a blazer and striped tee shirt, grinned at me. He looked exultant. I was speechless.

'You see why I was keeping the good wine till last,' she laughed. 'Isn't he delicious? Couldn't you just eat him up?'

I felt as if I'd received a blow in the stomach. I took the photo over to the Queen Anne sofa and sat down.

'You see,' Sybil was warbling, 'we met while you were in Japan. That's why he's such a surprise. We wanted to just slip away and do the deed and not tell anyone, which is a bit naughty, but I thought you really should know - not that we're having bridesmaids or anything like that.'

'Married?' I spluttered, 'You mean you're getting married to - him?'

'Yes dear. Isn't it exciting?' She sighed. 'I never expected anything like this to happen.'

I rose and went over to the mantelpiece.

'And I thought you meant . . .' I picked up the Chinese figure.

'Oh he's just for fun. Jason is for real.'

'Jason?' I quavered.

'Yes. That's his name. He's an angel. He simply adores me.' Her eyes swept the room. 'You know, he just loves this house.'

'And there was I thinking this was your new man.' Inwardly seething, I clenched the porcelain wise man.

Sybil giggled, 'Really, dear, you are a riot.'

I hissed, 'While all the time you were . . .'

'Careful dear. He's precious.'

But her words were too late. As I let the figure slip to the floor, Sybil watched in disbelief and horror. The crash made us both flinch.

'Now look what you've done.'

Her face turned a deathly pale.

'I didn't . . . I mean,' I stuttered my confusion.

'Don't bother to explain,' she sneered. 'You were always jealous of my things.'

'Don't be ridiculous,' I snapped. 'Why would I need any of your things?' I paused. 'Especially now.'

'Well in that case it's just as well.' Sybil gave a harsh little laugh. 'You see I was going to leave him to you. I thought - mistakenly it seems,' her voice wavered, 'that you appreciated fine things - that is, would appreciate him when I'm gone.'

I sat down on the regency sofa with the embroidered velvet cushions, avoiding the tapestry one, favoured by Sam.

'What do you mean gone? Where are you going for goodness sake?'

Sybil sighed, 'It doesn't really matter now.'

Languidly she waved her braceleted wrists over the remains of the porcelain figure.

'You mean . . .?'

'Yes, dear, I'm on my way Upstairs', she explained with a gracious smile, 'to the Great Siesta in the Sky.'

She sounded in such control. The hospital must be proud of her. That's something else they taught us on the programme. Control. As well as Timing Being Everything. I felt stifled. I was going to get an attack. If that happened then we'd see who'd be going first. Trust Sybil to want to win at everything. Even when it came to death. I glared at her. Serenely, she was now sweeping up the bits of the porcelain figure.

I sighed, 'Oh let me do that - please.'

She jingled her wrists at me. 'No. You've done enough harm as it is.'

'Oh Sybil! I'm so sorry.'

'Too late.' She sniffed, and continued to put the pieces into a dustpan.

'What can I do?'

'Do? You've done far too much. You and your - Arctic explorer! '

She rose regally from the floor and swept through the archway into the kitchen with the remains of her oriental wise man. I started to tidy the table.

'Desist,' she shrieked from the kitchen. 'Leave my things alone. That's your trouble. You never could leave things alone.'

There was a deathly silence. Eventually, Sybil took her place at the head of the table. And lifted the teapot.

'More tea?'

I shook my head.

'I'd like to say you'll still be more than welcome here - ,' she paused before flinging her final shot - 'but, of course, that will depend on Jason.'

And, in that moment I hated her, her house, her things. I resented the hospital for bringing us together. Most of all, I detested the blond man, who was taking her from me with a gloating smile. In my foolish rage I even hated Japan for giving him the chance of a lifetime. Not only was he stealing my friend, he was breaking our world into smithereens. And, he was depriving me of ever getting within an asses roar of the brass lamp with the map of India for a shade. For it was as clear as night follows day that he'd outlive me. He'd marry Sybil for her money, her things, her house. There'd be no more lovely chats. No more laughter. And, Sybil would never again pour strong brown tea into my cup, where a silver spoon stood upright, like a soldier.

Gypsy

I never wanted a party.

'We hardly know anyone,' I protested. 'It's far too soon.'

But Malachy wasn't having any. 'It pays dividends to be friendly to people,' he declared as he left for work. 'So I'm asking people round. Bill and Sally O'Hara are delighted. She suggested fancy dress.'

'You could at least have asked me first,' I fumed. 'As for fancy dress forget it! A roomful of adults all dolled up as *Bo Peep* and *Jack the Ripper* is completely out of the question.'

'Honestly Orla, if you're dead set against the idea, I can easily tell them at the office it's all off. Bill and Sally will understand.'

I could have screamed. 'And how in God's name can we do that with you and the O'Haras spreading the word right left and centre. Cancel my foot! We're stuck with it now.'

I might have guessed the party was Sally's idea. We'd barely arrived - just in the door - when she called. All chat and questions. Yap yap yap. On and on she went. I thought she'd never go.

I began to dread her visits. First it was cuttings for the garden then recipes for chutney. And those boring coffee mornings! Mind you the coffee wasn't as plentiful as the hard stuff. I don't know how they managed it out of the housekeeping. You should have heard them going on about their husbands. You'd think they were all married to Dracula! Malachy may not be God's Gift but I wasn't going to let the cat out of the bag at every gin swilling coffee morning. I tried to ward off Sally. A doomed hope as our husbands were now working together.

I resisted the fancy dress idea until a week later Sally called, breathless with excitement. 'Wait till you see what I've got here, Orla.' She tore at a brown paper parcel with red chipped nails. 'There's a wig as well.'

Pushing back a henna fringe badly in need of re-tinting, she placed raven pigtails on her head and held a Red Indian costume up against her. The effect was startling. That settled it. I wasn't going to be eclipsed by anyone at my own party.

Before you could say Bells at Bandon, the party night came. And there I was, adding the finishing touches to my gypsy make up and putting on my gold hoop earrings. Behind me in the bedroom mirror loomed Malachy, a pirate king, with the tucks of a frilled shirt skillfully arranged to hide his paunch.

First to arrive were the Donnellys in full golfing gear - without Fr. Pat for once. Jim produced a bottle of wine from the depths of his golfing bag.

'Here's to the new house. How brave having a

fancy dress party – and so soon after moving in.'

'It was Orla's idea,' replied Malachy, and disappeared to get glasses of the Welcome Cup.

My idea indeed!

The Donnellys jabbered on about the Captain's Prize and Fr. Pat's disappointment while we sipped our drinks. We'd had a few tasting sessions earlier of the Welcome Cup. Malachy said it was wiser to taste it beforehand as Bill's homemade wine varied considerably. Anyway we didn't want to get the guests maggoty the minute they arrived. When that happens it really spoils the fun.

The bell went and there they were. *John Wayne* and *Minnehaha*. Sally eyed me up and down.

'You look gorgeous. We came early to give a hand. If you need help at any stage of the proceedings just say the word.'

That's what I was afraid of.

'Everything's under control, Sally. Thanks all the same,' I said, steering her towards the drinks.

'Is everyone here? She shrieked. 'Oh! there's one of the Mahony twins. Charlie is it? You know Rory wouldn't speak to you since he got into the Junior Chamber of Commerce. '

The place filled up in no time. Malachy kept fidgeting with his eye patch every time the bell went in case he'd miss Henry, his boss. Sally kept dashing up to people shouting, 'How!' and giving an Indian salute. Some of the costumes were really

27

terrific. Like Noreen Power's. She was the living image of *Scarlett* in *Gone with the Wind*. Pity about her hair though. She could never do anything about it - even at school.

I chatted with Charlie Moore and his wife and then got involved with an Arab sheik. With all the background noise I couldn't catch his name. He refilled our glasses. The Welcome Cup wasn't half bad.

'Here's to us!' he laughed, and winked.

Through the doorway I could see Malachy in the conservatory waving at me before being swallowed up by a circus clown on stilts.

The sheik flicked back his headdress and whispered in my ear, 'We must have a tarantella before the night is out.'

Before I could reply the Murphys dressed as beggars appeared beside us.

'You look terrific Orla. Whatever made you think of fancy dress?' she asked.

'Yerra, cocktail parties can get boring,' I replied, 'But let me take a look at you. You make a fine pair of beggars.'

'God, we're not beggars Orla. We're South Sea Islanders. Sally whipped off our garlands upstairs and won't give them back.'

'Never mind. Come on now and chat to the Powers who're over there talking to a wizard.'

Through the doorway I could see Malachy in the conservatory laughing with one of the Three

Musketeers. People seemed to be getting on like a house on fire. I'd trouble announcing supper until the sheik hoisted me onto his shoulders to get everyone's attention. And supper was a roaring success. Everything got polished off even the fish paste sandwiches. If there's one thing I can't stand it's waste.

Pretty soon the floor was cleared for dancing and I got caught up in the whirl of things. Bill really knows how to dance - not like Malachy, who still can't put one foot in front of the other. Bill and I were having a drink to get our breath back when Sally veered over giving an Indian war cry that nearly deafened me.

'God! it's great fun Orla. Supper was delicious,' she shouted before seizing Bill and darting off on the warpath to the conservatory.

'Guess who?' asked a familiar voice.

As I turned around the sheik's eyes were glinting, headdress at a rakish angle.

'How's my gypsy moth? The gypsy baron is coming to get you but fear not the sheik of Araby will whisk you off to the secret delights of his desert retreat.'

He pulled me towards him. Better play it cool I told myself, trying to keep my voice level.

'Much as I'd love to see the desert my hands are tied and here I must remain.'

I looked over his shoulder for a glimpse of Malachy but couldn't see him anywhere among the tangle of costumes.

'No one argues with the sheik of Araby. I must have my way with you. You're irresistible.'

'And I'm on my way upstairs,' I gulped.

His eyes looked deeply into mine. 'Then I'll keep vigil here until my gypsy moth returns. Hurry back, you wondrous creature.'

When I waved at him from the landing, he was gazing up at me with a dreamy expression.

I made sure to dilly dally in the bathroom. There was a knock on the door. Thank God it was Noreen.

'Orla, open the door. This costume is killing me.'

I let her in. She was roasting in her outfit and fanned her face with her hand.

'Yerra, take it off for a minute and cool down.'

We undid the dress, underskirt and stays. It was the real thing all right. Noreen was always a stickler for detail.

'How did they manage in these clothes?' she gasped. 'No wonder Scarlett had such a hard time.'

I laughed and went into the bedroom. I was parched for a drink. As I glanced in the mirror to put on more lipstick I saw I was not alone. The sheik was behind me flourishing a bottle and two glasses. Just what I needed. A drink.

Things got a bit hazy after that. The sheik was a scream. He had me in stitches. Then for some unknown reason we were arguing about begonias. Yes that's right. Begonias. He tried to persuade me to take his cuttings.

'No way,' I protested, 'I'm allergic to cuttings.'
He didn't like that.

'If you refuse you insult me. And no one insults the sheik of Araby.'

'First time for everything' I said, and gave him a playful slap.

'Slap and tickle time eh?' he chortled, slapping me back. Like it was a party game.

'Stop!' I roared but he was so caught up in it all that he kept at it. That was when I seized the alarm clock from the bedside table and hit him on the head. He didn't stir, so I replaced his headdress, thinking he might as well wake up in one piece.

Downstairs Malachy was looking flushed. He took me by the arm.

'Where were you? The Murphys are gone and you weren't here to see them off.'

'Oh, just get me a drink, will you. '

I gulped it down. I never needed one more. Before I could tell Malachy about the sheik people came up to say Goodbye. Then I heard Sally calling out.

'Orla, join in the strip poker. Come on, let your hair down.'

I'm confused about what happened next. The last thing I remember was Sally dancing a tango with Malachy.

I never got a chance to tell him what happened. When I woke up I was on the sitting room sofa covered with a blanket. My head nearly burst as I tried to sit up. It was then I realised that I hadn't a stitch on. I went cold. An ear splitting sound made me jump. The phone. It was Sally. On and on she went. Yap yap yap.

'Orla, I just had to thank you for the smashing party. Wasn't the strip poker a riot? I nearly died when Charlie's turn came. His wife is a terrible pain though isn't she? God you were great fun yourself - once you got going. How's your head? I feel fine. We always keep plenty of Alka-Seltzer in the house - just in case.'

My head throbbed as I looked around. The place was a shambles. Nothing seemed to make sense.

Sally's voice rasped, 'Henry's wife just rang. She sounded panicky. Probably too much of your Welcome Cup. Old Henry's a bit of an eejit but nice enough - for a boss. I didn't get a chance to talk to him all night. Did you? He was the one dressed like something out of *The Desert Song*. . .'

I opened my mouth but no words came out.

'Orla, are you listening. . . Orla?

As I replaced the receiver I sensed there was someone else in the room. Through the doorway staggered the sheik of Araby. He looked sheepish and had a bruise as big as an egg on his forehead.

'Where am I? Is that you, my gypsy moth'? he quavered.

I stood up stiffly, holding the blanket to me as a shield.

'Bollocks to your begonias,' I said with all the dignity I could muster, and pointed to the front door.

He went quietly enough.

Malachy got promoted soon after the party. I never told him the whole story. I mean what's the point now that that we're moving on?

Just Like Home

Angela is listening to the interval talk on Radio Three. The woman's voice sounds affectionately humorous, now surprised, then nostalgic, as she outlines the changes in New York City over the past fifteen years. Angela knows what · she's talking about. Like the speaker, she's experienced for a short while the same thrill of living on the edge, being part of the artistic life of the East Village, on the brink of something new and daring. The shock of the unexpected always around the corner like coming face to face with a convoy of Hell's Angels on gleaming steeds, booted and spurred, revving up with the might of Armageddon outside the HA world headquarters. She, too, has savoured classic films at Theater 80, then a legendary local cinema. Oisín, her cousin's child, worked there as a projectionist. And, like the speaker, when facing into Alphabet City where street names start from A and go downhill from B, Angela has felt at first hand the same sense of danger.

Over a decade ago she'd visited Manhattan for the first time, staying with the professor in Garden City for a few days before taking up Oisín's offer of a bed at his place.

Gliding in the professor's green Volvo from his home, a haven of garden leafiness, to the deep dense jungle of the Lower East Side, where Oisín lived, they'd driven along hot streets full of litter and petrol fumes, passing people with faces the colour of coffee, chocolate, toffee and cocoa. When they reached Eldridge St. the professor pulled up outside Oisín's front door. She looked forward to seeing him again, remembering family holidays in Ballybunion; Lanky Oisín with his lopsided grin, building sandcastles and fishing for crabs. She remembered kissing better his jellyfish stings and teaching him the dog's paddle. It was hard to believe that he was now fully grown, had left Kerry behind and was finding his way in New York.

On the corner of Houston and Eldridge stood a Spanish grocery, on the opposite corner a Pet shop with signs in the window: *Get Your Pets Tested Here. Say Goodbye To Fleas.* The professor pointed out the finest Knish Bakery in New York - Yonah Schimmel's at 137 East Houston. Across the street an Afghanistan deli flanked a Korean drapery. Angela felt she'd arrived in the melting pot of a subcontinent.

After the professor left, she phoned Oisín at Theater 80 in St. Marks Place. Rory, his friend, explained that Oisín was away camping in the Badlands and arranged to meet her with the apartment keys outside the Catholic Church on Second Avenue. A meeting place she could hardly miss. And chosen for that reason, not because he was a religious maniac. Far from it, he assured her.

Rory had a shock of ginger hair and was dressed in black leather from head to toe. He handed her the keys. With the roar of traffic they both had to shout.

'Will Oisín be back soon?' He shrugged. 'He's on his own so who knows?' He laughed. 'Don't worry. You'll get the hang of things before you know it. Look, TRIBECA is the TRIangle BEfore CAnal St. and SoHo means South of Houston. Get it?'

She held out a white plastic bag. 'I brought rashers from home.' Rory's eyes widened. 'Magic! Oisín's a vegetarian but I'm a slave to the rasher. Thanks. You're a pal. Have to fly.' He took the bag. 'Oh, by the way, you're to have the bedroom. And if you find the Viennese Konditorei make sure you try their strawberry tarts. Fantastic.'

'Where is it?'

'Near Theater 80. You can't miss it. The scent is haunting.'

He waved and crossed the street, the white bag bobbing and weaving as he was swallowed up by a flock of dark figures. Their cigarettes pricked the dusk like glow-worms.

The scent of pizza lured her into the Afghanistan deli where young men with almond eyes played backgammon. The older ones sat alone, their gnarled fingers busy with worry beads. As she entered she could feel their curious glances. Traffic thundered by while she ate a slice of pizza and drank a can of diet Coke. On her way back to the apartment she hurried by a patch of withered grass where shadowy figures crouched on benches. 'Smokes? smokes?' a voice whispered. It was dark as she passed the subway at Houston and Second Avenue. An acrid smell rising from the entrance made her catch her breath.

She climbed the stairs to Oisín's apartment. The door next to it was partly open and without lock or handle. Through the chink she glimpsed an unmade bed and beer cans on the floor. From within a dark rich voice was singing:

'De Devil is a woman and de woman has got mah soul.

De devil is a woman and de woman has got control.'

Oisín's place was simple and surprisingly tidy. A futon took up most of the living room. On the bedroom floor there was a mattress with a Bart Simpson duvet cover. Between the bed and the window, plastic milk crates held a collection of jazz records, all neatly stacked. Her cousin had mentioned he was keen on jazz. There were no curtains. Instead a screen of latticed metal pressed against the windows, through which she caught glimpses of rooftops and fire escapes. In the tiny kitchen jars of beans and lentils stood tidily on shelves. Angela unpacked, putting clothes onto hangers, which she managed to squeeze into a cupboard already overstuffed. She put her books on the bedroom floor beside the mattress.

Sliding under the duvet she tried to doze but the honking of cars and sirens made rest impossible. Sitting up, she opened *Love in the Time of Cholera* and tried to read. But she couldn't concentrate. The bare window with its metal screen made her feel exposed. Like an animal in a cage. She turned off the light and lay down. She'd flown into New York three days ago. Only yesterday she'd been walking on Long Island beach with the professor. He had quoted snatches of Robert Frost as they'd gathered shells, the ocean stretching all the way to Ireland.

Suddenly she noticed a dark figure silhouetted against her window. Was her imagination playing tricks? Clutching the duvet, she forced herself to take a closer look. Outside on the fire escape standing with his back to her was a man. As if in slow motion, he held up a cigarette before leisurely sliding it to his lips. She watched as he ambled to and fro, exhaling indolently like a character in her South American novel taking the hacienda air with languorous ease. He still had his back to her with his head inclined towards the street below. But what if he turned around? Her heart pounded. She closed her eyes and prayed. When at last she opened them mercifully the figure had disappeared.

As she went to the kitchen to make coffee the sound of the doorbell startled her. She tiptoed into the living room. The bell rang again.

'Hi this is Henry from next door. Ah jes wonderin' if yuh was okay?'

A deep voice rich as dark chocolate resounded on the landing. She opened the door to find a tall black man grinning from ear to ear.

'If yuh need anythin' anythin' at all jes let me know.'

'Thank you, I'm fine.' She tried to sound calm, in control.

'Yuh shuh?'

'Yes.'

'Dat's all ah need ta know.'

She showered and put on a pink candy striped nightie. The touch of the cool cotton was soothing. But as soon as she lay down again, from the floor below came the sound of Latin American dance music. Throbbing rhythms pulsated through her. Rumbas. Sambas. She might as well be at a carnival in Buenos Aires. When the music stopped, as if on cue, the street doorbell rang.

'Who deah?' Henry's voice thundered through the intercom like surf breaking on a Caribbean island.

'It's me Henry and I wanna -' the thin voice of a young man floated back on the intercom.

'Ah's busy now.'

'Ken we come back later?'

'Deah's no party on heah, man.'

Angela sat up in bed and reached for a paperback about screenwriting. Before she could open it there was another ring at the street door.

'It's me again, Henry.'

The same thin voice on the intercom.

'Then whaddya hangin' around foh? Git yuh ass on up heah quick.'

With a lurching sound the front door opened. She heard footsteps on the stairs, then outside on the landing. Henry's rich throated laugh echoed through the house like a gushing waterfall. Visitors came and went next door. She was still on Page One of *Writing Screenplays That Sell*. Eventually the stream of callers ebbed away.

Then at last the key turned in the lock and it was Oisín. Now a grown man, he was taller, still lanky and with the same lopsided grin that reminded her of Ballybunion. And as chatty as ever.

'Angela, it's great to see you.' He hugged her. 'That nightie makes you look like a stick of candy,' he laughed.

'Oisín am I glad you're back. Look - it's - there's a man outside my window.' Her words tumbled out in a rush.

'Oh that's just Henry. Don't mind him. He's pretty weird but we get on OK. He likes to keep an eye out.'

'Oh? '

'Yeh, he likes to watch what happens on the street. Who comes into the house - that kind of thing.'

'Why? - and his door - it's broken. What's wrong with it?'

'He keeps getting busted. Don't look so worried.' He handed her a baseball bat. 'Here, take this. Wake me if you hear anything.'

She eyed the baseball bat with distaste.

'No, you keep it.'

Oisín regarded her carefully.

'Did he peer in at you?'

'No but-' Angela bit her lip.

'There you are, harmless.' He went into the kitchen. She could hear water running. 'Angela, you're going to love it here,' he called out. 'We're right beside the F train. That's the beauty of this place.'

She heard him whistling, then asked, 'How was it in the Badlands?'

'Brillo. Forgot my supplies but dried food did the trick.'

Suddenly she felt ashamed. Here she was fretting about herself when Oisín, who'd left the Boy Scouts at 14, could have perished, out alone under the stars in a foreign land.

'By the way,' he added nonchalantly as he came back from the kitchen with tea, 'Henry is a pimp but don't worry.'

'Don't worry?'

'Harmless like I said.' He grinned. 'Just steer clear of any late night callers.'

At last she slept. In her dream she was standing, murder weapon in hand, staring down at her victim. The man lay in a pool of blood that clotted his black curly hair. His face was turned away but she knew that it was Henry. Shocked, she dropped the gory baseball bat at the sound of sirens coming to take her away.

She awakened to blaring sirens and flashing lights.

'What's up Oisín?'

'Same old thing. Go back to sleep.'

In the morning he made her a cup of apple and cinnamon tea. Afterwards he washed the cups and put them away, explaining that all traces of food must be cleared up immediately to discourage the roaches. But they were harmless. And she was not to worry. The main thing was to keep her money safe. She showed him her money belt.

'Good stuff. I use the icebox. You can put your valuables in there if you like.' She nodded. As he headed for the door he advised, 'On the streets look no one in the eye, and avoid Needle Park. It's along Houston near Yonah Schimmel's and full of druggies.' It sounded like the place she'd passed last evening. He grinned. 'Get the hang of the subway and you'll be laughing.'

On the corner of Houston and Second Avenue Angela walked by a fenced in playground where sloe eyed children in frilly dresses were playing. Their tight curls were scraped up from their heads and tied with bright ribbons. Through the fence they looked like tropical birds in a Zoo. She crossed the street, hurrying past foul smelling bundles of rubbish and old clothes on waste ground. When two of the bundles stirred she realised they were people. Shocked, she moved further along to where a man was spreading blankets and setting up shop. He was trying to sell detergent, hairbrushes and socks. No one seemed to be buying. At a café called Elvis's Place she sipped a cappuccino. *Jailhouse Rock* thundered from the jukebox. On First Avenue, she passed an old black woman, who shouted, 'Whaddya starin' at?' Angela had forgotten to look into the middle distance.

She darted into the nearest shop. Spirals of incense wafting upwards made her sneeze. She picked up a Birthday card, glancing at its lurid message before replacing it swiftly on the rack.

'We come to buy, not to touch,' shrieked a young man with hair the colour of magenta and painted fingernails to match.

People turned to stare at Angela. She pretended to study a collection of oriental fans next to a garish poster hanging behind a display of small blue bottles. A girl in studded black leather pushed past her and picked up one of the bottles. In bold letters it proclaimed, *Bottled Love Potion - Results Guaranteed.*

'We don't like people touching things,' the magenta haired youth shrieked. The girl shrugged and left. Angela bought a jokey card for Oisín.

'Have a gay day,' the youth warbled, handing her the change. Outside the shop she realised what he'd said and laughed.

She had her first taste of the subway when she took the F train uptown for her lecture. A stench rising from the murky depths at Second Avenue made her gasp. Her stomach heaved as she picked her way down the steps over a huddle of bodies. On the dimly lit platform she clutched her bag tightly, feeling the money belt snug against her waist.

Before her lecture on Fifth Avenue she went to the Magritte exhibition at the Metropolitan Museum of Art. She particularly liked the picture of a steam train emerging from a fireplace.

People at her lecture were shocked to learn Angela was staying on the brink of Chinatown.

'I'd move out if I were you,' a man warned. 'One and half murders every MINUTE.'

A woman whispered, 'Get off the subway at Union Sq. and take a cab the rest of the way.'

She did but Oisín was not impressed. 'For Chrissake, Angela, you meet the same people on the F train uptown as down here.' He frowned.

'Look, you're quite safe in the bedroom. Nothing can get through your window's steel gate.'

'What about a gun?'

'No chance.'

'Or an arrow?'

He laughed, 'If you see Robin Hood, just call.'

The heat in the bedroom was stifling.

'Open the window if you're hot,' Oisín called out from the living room.

'No, no I'm fine'

'Just a crack. He's not a lizard.'

Wild horses wouldn't make her open the window. She fixed a makeshift curtain with a bedspread she'd bought at the Korean drapery. In bed she tossed fitfully. Finally she drifted off. In her dream she was on the F train, trying to enter the fireplace in Magritte's painting.

'Breakfast time,' Oisín announced next morning as bottles clattered on the stairs. Angela peered out onto the landing. A black man was bringing a crate of Heineken into Henry's.

That night she jerked awake. From next door came the sound of crashing furniture, then a woman's voice pleading. Angry voices tore at her. Through the wall she could hear Henry roaring, 'Go way, man. Dis aint de circus.' Louder crashing noises were followed by a sudden silence. Then she heard the sound of weeping. 'Gimme mah money,' a woman's voice pleaded. Angela wanted to thump the wall and yell, *Henry, pay the woman*. But of course she did no such thing.

Next day, when she suggested reporting Henry to the Police, Oisín shrugged and told her that the cops didn't care.

'But this woman is working hard. They're cheating her,' Angela protested.

'Probably stoned.'

'She still needs her pay.'

'Don't let them get to you. I sleep on my side, ears muffled by Bart and my pillow. That way you don't get the full brunt of it.' He smiled. 'Try it.'

The following night she woke at 4.am, hearing in the pause between sirens a squeaking noise from the kitchen. It sounded like someone squeezing a plastic washing up container. Surely Oisín wasn't cleaning the kitchen at this hour?

He was startled to see her out of bed. 'It's okay. You're not to be afraid. The rats are Henry's problem.'

Angela gasped, 'Rats? But – but - my bed is on the floor.'

'I know.' He spoke calmly as if soothing a troubled toddler. 'But they won't come near us. Those rats belong to Henry. They're under his floorboards.'

A kind of controlled hysteria seized her. A feeling now associated with life on the Lower East Side. A feeling that was becoming all too familiar.

While Oisín clambered in under Bart Simpson's protective mantle, Angela stuffed cotton wool in her ears to distance the squeakings and scurryings under the bedroom floor. When she fell asleep it was to dream of an army of rodents marching under Yonah Schimmel's Knish Bakery. She awoke sweating just as they reached Eldridge St.

After that she made a habit of eating takeaways off waxed paper, carefully disposing of crumbs. Apart from the pests her subconscious was grappling with, there were roaches. Black and shiny. Creeping from crevices.

She could hardly believe that a few days ago she'd been discussing her lecture plans with the professor in the seclusion of his book lined study and driving to the university in a green Volvo. Now when she descended the steps to the F train, those huddled bodies aroused in her strong feelings of revulsion and pity. How could anyone ever get used to it?

Then a notice appeared in the lobby with the black words PEST CONTROL in block letters, proclaiming to all that Henry's apartment was being fumigated.

'Told you not to worry.' Oisín winked at her. 'You can open the window now.'

Life at Eldridge St. took a turn for the better. Things became quieter next door, with no more cries from the pleading woman. Angela made herself open the bedroom window. Just a crack.

'She's gone,' Oisín said one morning.

'Hope she's getting paid.'

Angela was getting to know her way around the area. She discovered an Egyptian café filled with dark skinned workers where you ate deliciously aromatic lunches for next to nothing. At the Viennese Konditorei she found gorgeous fruit tarts with whole strawberries lying on top of pureed fruit like jewels in a casket. She bought some for Rory who was nearby at Theater 80. When he saw them his eyes lit up.

'I'd crawl across Brooklyn Bridge and all the way into town for one of these,' he sighed.

As the reality of the Lower East Side took over, Angela's brief stay at the professor's seemed like a mirage. When he phoned he might have been calling from another planet.

'Are you all right?' His tone was worried.

'Sure I am.'

'Good. I just thought after last night's murder on your street -'

'What?' Angela was more puzzled than shocked.

'Didn't you hear the sirens?'

'Oh those. They're part of the scenery now. '

She felt curiously untouched by the fact that someone had been killed on her very doorstep. Was she getting callous?

The following evening by the time she'd finished her lecture near Central Park it was twilight so she hailed a cab.

'The nearest subway please.'

The driver guffawed. 'Thirty dollar bill? Aint you got nothin' smaller?'

He drove off in a squeal of brakes, leaving her in the softly falling darkness.

'Pay no mind, ma'am. Folk in New York got no gentility.' A voice purred at her side. A well dressed man. She hadn't felt him creeping up on her. 'Subway's coupla blocks along thatta way.' He smiled, a gleam of teeth in the dark.' And watch out for muggers.'

She turned gratefully towards the subway.

'Thanks, I will.'

Suddenly a glancing blow to her back knocked her breathless, flinging her to the ground. She caught a glimpse of feet in sandals and torn socks. A hairy arm bent down, and whipped her bag away as her fingers twitched helplessly. In the fading light she could barely make out the shapes of her assailant and the well dressed man running into the park.

It was all over as swiftly as it began. Stumbling to her feet, she called out. Her voice faltered hopelessly towards the park where someone was playing a guitar. She felt for the money belt near her ribs. Still there thank God. Somehow she reached the subway and anxiously scanned the track for signs of the F train. At last it came. Entering the carriage was like boarding a gilded chariot to Tir na nOg.

'Good ole F train,' Oisín chuckled when she got back. 'Guess what I found in the ice box?'

He held up a small rectangular packet wrapped in plastic. Her passport. Angela laughed, feeling the waves of tension beginning to dissolve.

Henry was singing next door. 'De devil is a woman and de woman has got mah soul.'

Oisín asked, 'Prefer Elvis's Place for coffee?' The voice rich as dark chocolate sang on.

'De devil is a woman and de woman has got control.

Go, go, go, go way, woman, set me free -'

Oisín grinned at her. 'Well? She grinned back.

'No here is fine. Just like home.'

That was over a decade ago. Ten years before Ground Zero. An eternity. Angela's work has taken her to Europe, South Africa & Australia but she hasn't returned to New York, where Oisín now works for a prestigious Manhattan art gallery. He's married with a young family and living happily in a brand new apartment – in Eldridge St. – of all places.

On Radio Three the woman ends her talk and the concert resumes. Angela smiles to herself. Maybe it's time to go back.

Pusakis at Paros

If you want to meet the Paros pusakis, take the winding road from Parikia where the ferries land, and cross the island to Drios. It's simple - once you know how. Just wend your way down through Podromos and Lefkes until you get to Drios village. When you arrive, ask for Nissiotiki Spiti. You reach it by going down a dusty path, passing the Anchor Taverna on your right and an ancient dovecote on your left. At the end of the path you're there. It looks more like a private house than a small hotel. Just walk through the gate painted that deep blue of the Cyclades, to match the shutters, and enter the garden, where cascades of bougainvillea glint in the sun like clusters of purple jewels. Go around the corner of the house. And there, glimpsed through a profusion of scarlet hibiscus, is the sea. An endless expanse of sparkling turquoise. Majestic, serene. Perfect. The place exudes peace. No mechanical sounds of any kind. And no transistors. None. The pusakis don't like them. For sheer *kefi*, these creatures of taste and discernment are a leap ahead of the languorous cats of Crete. But I forget myself. Wherever there are free spirits, there is no contest.

That first morning, we breakfast on honey and yoghurt under a tamarisk tree. I gaze out at the islands. Hazy shapes emerge, shimmering in the heat, dissolve and disappear. I look towards Naxos, and think of Nora, asking us to stay. *Next time,* we promised. Only there wasn't a next time.

A black cat appears on a low wall between our table and the sea. I offer yoghurt while G tries to interest a tortoiseshell mother and her family in some bread. Two white kittens tumble into the group, who wait patiently while we drink our coffee. They consume the remains of our yoghurt, and scamper off into a tangle of trailing greenery.

We give our cats Greek names, like Plato, Sappho, Orpheus. Plato, alas, manifested none of his namesake's greatness. A weedy little thing, he loved to immerse himself, most uncatlike, in pools of water. Perhaps he was meditating on the meaning of Life. All too soon, despite reviving drops of cognac in his milk, he departed Lethewards to taste the Stygian darkness.

Sappho came to us in a friend's pocket one autumn evening. She was a tabby, wise with gleaming eyes and more a philosopher than a poet. When she gave birth in our bedroom, her purring woke me in the night. I crept out of bed, moving gently towards the sound. Four tiny kittens were huddling in her fur. She purred as if she'd got the Nobel Prize for Feline Motherhood. Perhaps my delight in this miracle gave her ideas. She would bring the kittens to our bed for safe keeping while she resumed her nocturnal meanderings. In her own way she helped me mourn. After my mother's death, I found it hard to cry. Really weep. Six months later, Sappho was killed by a motorist outside our Dublin house. It was only then the tears came. I wept as if there was no to-morrow.

At the beach, I glance at the book G is reading. On the cover a huge eye, like a balloon, is floating up, up and away. I lie back, soaking in the sun, a slave to Helios. I listen to the sea. To an islander, reared at the edge of the Atlantic and caught in its roar, the sound of gentle waters is always a surprise. Later, while G is swimming, I pick up his book, lying face down in the sand. On the back, is the caption for Odilon Redon's image on the cover. *The Eye Like a Strange Balloon Mounts Towards Infinity.* Reading those words, I think of Nora. A free spirit.

As I write in the garden at Nissiotiki Spiti, the black kitten seems to have adopted me. It plays with my notes, scampering under the pine tree chasing pages. This tiny jaguar is like Orpheus, a gleaming beauty of a black panther, who wandered into our lives, as cats do.

During the glorious reign of Orpheo Negro, Jupiter landed. A large - a very large white bunny. His sharp teeth could bite through anything. In a house of free spirits, he was treated the same as everyone else, i.e. fed and then let off. However, when Bunny was discovered under the breakfast table munching away at G's only good pair of leather shoes, he was banished from the house. In the garden he hopped about happily but would dash over and spray my legs whenever I used the clothesline.

'It's all right Mum, he just thinks he's your husband,' my daughter consoled.

To escape, I was forced to dart out under enemy fire, do my business and nip back inside before he did his. It was a race to the death. We built a run for Bunny. Afterwards I had such sweet moments, hanging out the washing while he sped up and down, eating the place to bits. When he developed abscess after abscess on his left side, the vet feared Jupiter might be facing his final leap to the Great Rabbit Hutch in the Sky. I was appointed Chief Nurse. However, administering medicaments proved fraught. As he languished, I fixed my gaze on his perfect right side, white and fluffy and resplendent.

In the hushed night, the only sounds are gentle swishing sounds of the sea. Not a pusaki to be seen or heard. They are off at the tavernas, charming diners. The garden is full of fragrant silence. Overhead a milky band stretches across the heavens. I go out onto the little balcony for a breath of air and lean against the railings, painted that deep blue of the Cyclades. A sickle moon hovers over Naxos. The pine tree whispers in the scented breeze. I feel like flying out over the sea.

Our next feline - the only one without a Greek name - approached via *The Evening Press.* "Good Home Wanted for Black and White Male Cat. Otherwise will have to be put down." No sooner had the words leapt off the page than we were dialling the Cat Rescue People. They were guarded. An outdoor cat mightn't settle. There followed an inquisition, that was insulting to cat people like ourselves. Did someone think we were about to eat the creature or use it in some bizarre sacrifice? All we wanted was to save the animal from certain death. Little did we realise that we would be leading it towards a fate worse than death by Holy Orders. But I digress.

The cat arrived. Very very large, with a pretty face and enormous feet. Black like Orpheus and white with a pink nose like Jupiter. The cat's foster mother tearfully delivered him and promised to phone. At the time, our daughter, who has an instinct for wild things, was taming a hedgehog. When this prickly visitor emerged late one night from under the stairs, she fed it bread soaked in milk. It honoured us with a few visits, and then disappeared to work its way under the houses of Dublin 6. It could well be in Wicklow by now.

At first, Pussy scuttled under the stairs in the direction of our disappearing hedgehog and could only be coaxed out by our daughter, who talked to him in cat language. This worked wonders. He inched his way up the hall and through the study door to the strains of *The Moonlight Sonata* only to hide under my desk. Was he trying to tell me something? Beethoven however, seemed to have a calming effect.

The Cat Rescue People advised keeping him indoors for six weeks. On the third day we opened the window and let him off. After all, we are a house of free spirits. Two days later he was still on his travels. Being cat lovers, we confidently awaited his return. His foster mother bore the news of his absence bravely and suggested making bird noises to lure him back, giving a bravura demonstration over the phone. She even offered to come over and repeat the performance since I was unwilling to imitate her warblings. I graciously declined her offer. On the third day Pussy returned without the benefit of birdcalls, to his foster mother's shock and relief. He soon settled. Rolling in the grass and chasing wild things were among his delights. With his black and white fur he seemed like Orpheus and Jupiter rolled into one. Half cat, half rabbit. Sometimes we called him the cabbit, which was irreverent. Perhaps this was why he fell prey to the ministrations of the archdeacon's housekeeper and took Holy Orders. But that's another story.

I walk by the water. Like any islander, I'm always looking outwards and onwards to the next sea voyage, to the far shore. Sipping ouzo at a harbour kafenion, I sit with my back to the setting sun. I am facing east. Naxos is behind me. It's only a short boat journey but I cannot bear to go there. Not now.

On our last night we go to a taverna on the waterfront. We take the table, where a piece of paper, fluttering in the breeze, proclaims TZAK in boldly pencilled letters. Nearby a group of Germans drink beer. Recognising them from the beach, we exchange smiles. A family of pusakis gathers as we feast, gazing out beyond the harbour to the sea. Caiques, clustered near the tiny white church on the pier, rock gently in the water. Jack's wife throws bread to the fish while I feed the kittens. Listening to Jack playing Rembetiko airs on the bouzouki, I remember his daughter singing the same songs as we drifted over the wine dark sea to Sifnos. At the next table, a boy of eight with glistening eyes turns to face the music, sitting astride the back of his chair like a man.

'Er ist begeistert,' murmurs one of the Germans as the child's fascinated gaze is held by the power of Jack's playing. The boy's father, sending over tributes of retsina, hums to the melodies while Jack and his beautiful Slavic wife think of their nightingale daughter at music college in London.

The Germans leave. A small black cat hovers at the harbour's edge.

'Ela, pusakimou' I call softly.

It glides over and graciously accepts bits of fish.

'Orea', I smile, patting its sleeky fur and offer a piece of G's souvlaki, filched from his plate. A last offering - till next time. Will there be a next time?

Back home in Dalkey, the bottle of Trebbiano'97 comes in an ice bucket. Fancy for a pub. By some miracle it's sunny and we eat outdoors. I lift my glass. The chilled wine is crystal clear with a pale silvery green tinge. It looks like the waters of Paros. They say in Greece that wine delights all the senses except hearing so we tap our glasses on the table before clinking them together.

'Sigia!'

And, when we drink, it's like diving into the Aegean. Would there be a next time?

At home we play music and read. G picks up *Captain Corelli's Mandolin*. It's my turn now for *Enduring Love*. I'm fascinated by that picture of an eye like a balloon on the cover.

Putting a CD in the player, I realise that most of our music has the Naxos label. Once more I think of Nora.

Remember, if you want to meet the Paros pusakis, make sure you stay at Nisiotiki Spiti. I promised Grigoriou I'd spread the word. But not to everyone. Just to people like ourselves. Antitransistorite cat lovers, longing for peace and the magic of Greece.

His Darling

She wasn't beautiful or elegant like the girls he'd admired, even worshipped, when he was twenty. But she was his Deirdre. And, always crystal clear about the women in his life - even in the early days - whenever he fell for a girl it was final.

Like his wife. Poor Mona. His darling till the day of her death, and for a long time afterwards. He'd always been protective towards Mona and wanted to bring her home from hospital so he could mind her himself. The doctor, however, told him firmly she'd be better off with proper medical care. Meaning he was incapable of minding his own wife and now would he please mind his own business and let the doctors get on with theirs. This only intensified his desire to protect her in her final struggle, driving him to placate the nurses with gifts, waylay the doctor for extra snippets of information and fiercely guard Mona from unwelcome visitors.

His sister was the worst offender. She'd arrive by stealth, creep into Mona's private room, jabber away about Reverend Mother's plans to renovate the convent or other such nonsense, and exhaust his wife, whose suffering was now on display for visitors. For a visitor was all his sister would ever be. They hadn't been a close family. Not such a bad thing. It meant that when he met and captured Mona he could devote his entire heart to her. She was breathtaking with her blue laughing eyes and bobbed hair. And what a voice! No wonder she was in constant demand at musical evenings. And what's more she could play the piano with finesse. As if tasting a vintage claret, he savoured the memory of those days when the house rang with music and laughter.

He poured a cup of tea. Plenty for one in the tiny teapot. After Mona died he'd sorted out the kitchen, using one place setting to save the good china. He stored her hoard of rice, lentils, tea, and tall brown bags of sugar in the top kitchen press, safe out of harm's way. What a divil for hoarding she was!

'You'll be glad of what's on the top shelf,' she often joked.

Afterwards he hadn't the heart to interfere with her store of dried goods. However, when his sister swooped in 'to help' she discovered weevils in the rice and chastised him for harbouring germs. How dare she stand tiptoe on Mona's kitchen steps and peer into the Holy of Holies! He'd given her a right roasting for interference. Since that day she hadn't darkened his door, something for which he'd be eternally grateful.

After Mona's death people pitied him because he had to cook and clean for himself. They didn't know that menial tasks kept him sane when the ache in his heart became too great. He'd lived with the ache so long it now seemed part of him. At first when the wound was raw and smarting he'd clung to it as the one true feeling in his life. Then, when it dulled, he grew fearful that the only real part of her he possessed would disappear, leaving him to his solitary cups of tea and lonely evenings. He felt guilty when the wound became less sensitive to the touch. Gradually the nagging ache lessened. And then, one day, it was as if she had finally left.

He decided to sell the house and contacted an estate agent. He was expecting a crisp young man, eager for a quick sale. However, a pleasant looking girl arrived instead, neat and trim with her briefcase. They hit it off right away. She wanted to know why he was selling and went around the house touching things in a proprietary way that told him she knew quality when she came across it. He could see her approving glance giving the French clock the once over. He offered her a glass of the wine he'd brought back from Portugal. When they met again he might produce his own *Chateau Lambay* and chat about the wine club. Lord, how Mona loved her wine!

'The way I see it,' she asserted, 'most people sell because they're forced to.'

He nodded. How right she was!

She laughed, 'I wouldn't want you selling for the wrong reasons.'

He was surprised by her candour.

'What about your commission?' he countered.

'Oh, I won't be with the firm much longer.' She sighed, 'I want to follow my dream.'

He refilled their glasses. 'Yes?'

During the pause that followed he waited in the absurd hope that she'd confide her dream to him, a perfect stranger. But that didn't come till later.

Over several visits Deirdre told him about herself. Her mother, who owned a small hotel down the country, needed her help during the busy season. As she craved independence, this was a cause of endless friction. So in order to avoid her mother's demands she'd ended up in the city, taking the first job on offer but felt stifled by the commercial side of the property business.

'I'd love to open my own hotel and cook for people myself,' Deirdre confided. He nodded appreciatively, impressed by her enterprising spirit. 'I'd make people feel at home,' she added with shining eyes.

'I'm sure you would,' he offered and was touched by the warmth of her smile.

Later she announced she was going to take evening classes in advanced cooking so that she'd be up to scratch for the challenge ahead.

He started having doubts about selling the house. Once someone began to express interest he found himself raising the asking price.

'Take your time,' Deirdre advised him.

Torn with the thought of moving to a strange place, he decided to take it off the market.

'I think you're doing the right thing,' she confirmed. 'Especially if your heart isn't in it.'

So overnight the *For Sale* sign was removed.

He took his crockery to the sink and cleared away the bread, butter and honey, dusting the crumbs near the sugar bowl that hadn't moved from the same spot since he took over the house. Mona was forever fidgeting with the kitchen, disturbing its order so that one week they ate facing the garden, the next with their backs to it. And, she couldn't keep a definite place for anything. He'd changed all that. Pleased, he noted the tidy sink, glinting draining board; marble topped table already set for his next meal, and felt the presence of order.

After he'd finished, from lifelong habit, he brushed his teeth. No fillings and every tooth in his head. Not like Mona. Lord, how she loved chocolates! Her eyes would light up whenever he'd bring her favourite box of Double Centres or bars of Toblerone.

At first she used visit him in his dreams every night, then less frequently. Often she was in green velvet and wore long silver earrings that dangled. She was as he had first known her - beautiful and beyond his reach – as she was now. When the dreams ceased he felt a new pang of guilt. The ache of her was gone, and then the dreams. He redoubled his efforts to lure her back, making a shrine of her picture in the sitting room, which he denuded of all other faces. In the evenings he'd keep vigil, sitting in the burgundy velvet armchair she'd so desperately wanted, though the house bulged with enough chairs to seat a regiment.

Even after he'd taken the house off the market Deirdre continued to call. He was flattered and looked forward to her visits. She brought a slow, easy warmth into the house, dropping in unexpectedly on her way into town to the theatre or cinema. Sometimes she'd turn up for tea, bringing a cake or apple tart, promising to surprise him with *haute cuisine* once her advanced cookery course ended. Scoffing at homely dishes like bacon and cabbage, she produced a book with pictures of mouthwatering dishes that she'd serve in her own hotel when the time was ripe. And, watching her gleaming eyes as she outlined her plans, he recognised her as a girl of spirit. If she wanted something she was sure to get it. He murmured approvingly over images of *Boeuf en croûte* and *Cassoulet*. When alone, however, he had to admit it was hard to beat a nice piece of collar of bacon. With the cabbage cooked in the bacon water. Wasn't he and the whole of Ireland reared on it? Indeed, it was now his mainstay unless he took the bus into town for lunch at Bradley's staff canteen, where he was treated like royalty, though he'd never worked there. Simply turning up and smiling at the waitress had done the trick.

After her course ended, Deirdre, who needed to practise her culinary skills, offered to cook for him if he wished to entertain. He was delighted and flattered. Mona's idea of gastronomic efforts had been a tray of savouries at their musical evenings. In contrast his dear girl hadn't a note in her head but she was a dab hand at dinner parties, and soon his carefully selected guests were dazzled by her *Beef Stroganoff* and *Crème brûlée*. He was ashamed to find himself comparing these dishes with Mona's plain cooking for he considered loyalty one of the cardinal virtues. But the Mona he knew in the old days, the laughing singing Mona, would understand that he had to survive as best he could in a dead house full of empty fireplaces and the sound of soccer on the telly. For too long he had brooded, and now, thanks to his dear girl, he was literally reborn.

People remarked on his zest for life. The invitations of well meaning neighbours tended to clash with Deirdre's visits. As an attempt to repay her generosity he took her out to dinner. Well dressed and attentive to his needs, she was captivating company. He fancied other men envied him his young lively companion. Before long he was alternating suppers at home with meals in the latest restaurants, where he often arranged that she'd inspect the kitchens. For she needed to keep abreast of culinary trends in order to follow her dream. Whenever he was invited anywhere he asked if he could bring his Deirdre, and pined if he had to go alone.

He could barely wait for evening when she would call with a surprise. He wondered what delight she was planning for him now. For Christmas it had been a brandy glass, the perfect match of one given by a member of the family last year.

In the bedroom he selected a tie he'd bought recently. A bold red with yellow stripes. He would wear the new tie pin. A man could be dead long enough.

'Love me, dee-ee-ee-rest, love me!' he sang while he combed his hair.

As he waited in the sitting room it struck him that a great part of the joy he derived from his dear girl lay in the sweet ache of anticipation. If she ever went away he'd miss that almost as much as her company. He turned on the telly - boon to the solitary. They'd bought it after Mona sold the piano. Lord, how she loved those weepy films! After watching a replay of highlights from a recent match he turned it off. The clock winked the remaining minutes at him. It was one of Mona's more successful buys. She was a terrible woman for bargains, always off to an auction down the country with one of her cronies. He'd shuddered when moth-eaten sofas, dressing tables or enormous wardrobes arrived by lorry, making their suburban home swell with furniture that belonged in a mansion. Yet, after she was gone he couldn't bring himself to remove her 'bargains.' And had to admit she had an eye for smaller items – like the French clock that kept perfect time, and was now ticking each minute until Deirdre's visit.

· He put two glasses on the mahogany coffee table and brought cheese and wine from the kitchen. She might be peckish. He eyed his preparations approvingly. Maybe she'd stay longer this time. He smiled, anticipating an amiable chat over several glasses of wine, even half hoping for a minor crisis in her life. For these crises provided welcome opportunities to comfort her. Like the time her car was broken into and her handbag stolen. On the phone her voice had sounded full of unshed tears.

'I don't know what to do. When I rang Daddy he ate the face off me.'

'Where are you?'

'At the flat.'

'Don't move. I'll be over in ten minutes and you can tell me all about it then.'

Replacing the receiver, he'd secretly admitted it was asking for trouble to leave a handbag unattended in a car. Then, blessing his good fortune, he'd dashed from his telly to shield her from adversity.

Over coffee it all spilled out.

'You see I was out in Howth - with the chap at work I told you about. On the spur of the moment we decided to go for a walk. You know how these things happen.'

He did indeed, and listened intently as she continued, 'We went to the end of the pier and didn't notice the time passing.' Her eyes clouding over, she went on, 'When we got back the car window had been smashed and my bag taken. He brought me home by taxi and went off to tell the guards.'

'Don't worry your head, darling. I'll sort everything out for you.'

With a neighbour's help he'd managed to tow her car back to his own garage where he minded it jealously till it could be repaired.

Mention of the chap at work opened up the possibility of some young fellow laying claim to his Deirdre. He realised, of course, that such a lively girl would be surrounded by admirers. Indeed, the conquest of hugging so much of her time and talent to himself was heightened by the prospect of capturing her from rivals. Soon afterwards, he was forced to acknowledge the existence of such a rival when she brought him along one evening. Her shining eyes made him wonder how involved she was with this nondescript fellow, who'd made her throw caution to the winds and leave her handbag in the car, a silly thing for a sensible girl to do.

'Heard such a lot about you, sir. It's a great pleasure.'

The fellow's tone was deferential, with the 'sir' trumpeting the gulf of years between them. Inwardly cursing the young man who could bring that gleam to her eyes, he'd made a special effort to be cheerful, exchanging pleasantries as they sipped drinks. Yet they'd barely arrived when it seemed they were off.

'What's your hurry?' he asked, trying to pour them another drink.

'Dan has an early start in the morning,' Deirdre explained.

So, in order that Dan might be fit for his early start, he'd gone for their coats. When he returned they were looking at Mona's picture.

'I was just saying that your wife must have been a very beautiful woman,' Dan offered.

'My wife was one in a million. A truly remarkable person.'

They'd stood for moment in silence, locked in their own thoughts.

Lately the young man hadn't been mentioned once in conversation, and by this time could well be out of the picture. *Out of sight, out of mind,* he thought gratefully as things slipped deliciously back into how they'd been before.

The clock ticked away. It was only a question of time now. He glanced around. Everything shipshape. He sang:

'Just a song at twilight when the lights are low,
When the flickering shadows softly come and go.
Though the heart is weary, sad the day and long,
Still to us at twilight comes –'

His heart fluttered as the bell rang. In the hall he hurriedly opened the door to his Deirdre. She had an unusual air of excitement about her.

'Come in, come in. Don't stand out here in the cold. Let me take your coat.'

He led her into the sitting room and offered cheese and wine.

'I've eaten, thanks, but I'd love a glass of wine.'

They were seated on the sofa that belonged in a mansion when she showed him the ring. For a moment he felt as if a punch had struck and winded him. And kept glancing from the cluster of diamonds to her face, unable to say anything.

'Isn't it gorgeous?' she breathed, admiring it with her eyes.

'Well, well, this is certainly a surprise,' he managed to say at last.

'I wanted you to be the first to know. Tell me, are you pleased? '

She was like a child telling a secret, eager and appealing, and looking into her eyes, he thought she'd never seemed so delectable and so beyond his reach.

'You know, my dear, there's no man at all who would be worthy of you.'

'Of course you'll be the first to be asked to the wedding. Golly, what a lot of things to do.'

As her eyes glazed over at the challenge ahead, he coughed, 'I suppose when you're married you'll soon forget all about your old friends.'

'Ah now,' she teased with a turn of the head that was at once perky and chiding, 'sure I couldn't possibly forget you.'

Just as he was about to pour more wine she covered the glass with her hand. The diamonds winked at him, and in that moment he hated the hard little glittering pieces that would never leave her finger.

'I'd love another glass, honestly, but I must go.'

In the hall he helped her into her coat.

'Call in soon again,' he commanded.

'I'm working down the country next week,' she replied.

'I'll miss you,' he sighed, 'You know I always love to see you.'

'Well, you'll have to wait till I get back,' she laughed before stepping through the hall door.

'Make it soon,' he urged, feeling a sudden rush of abandonment.

He waved her off down the garden path and in that gesture waved away his Deirdre as he had known her.

Alone in the silent house, he sang softly, 'When the flickering shadows softly come and go.'

Back in the sitting room he stood, glass in hand, looking at the French clock, and reflected that Mona's taste in clocks was exquisite.

Halloween in Manhattan

During that warm sunny October the Manhattan air is thick and hot with Presidential candidates. And, as I remember it, the professor introduces me to Elina at a reception following a lecture I gave at Columbia. Her credentials are most impressive. Working as a judge in the juvenile court, she's a known advocate of prisoners' rights while also campaigning for worthy causes on her own tv chat show.

'The way I see it,' she is to tell me later, 'I simply try to help the less fortunate - those considered *undesirables*.'

By the way she stresses the last word I get the impression she rates herself an angel of mercy. And, that first evening in Manhattan, she looks angelic with her sweet smile and periwinkle blue eyes. Smartly dressed in black, she's charming and flirty in an understated way, with a low voice and a habit of nonchalantly flicking back her dark swinging hair. We chat about my theatre work with prisoners back home and she promises to introduce me to the Head of Film at NYU. Then, as if struck by a sudden idea, she announces that she wants to take me off and make a film.

'About what?' I ask intrigued.

'Darling, it's not about any *thing*,' answers Elina, who's now purring like a kitten.

'Oh?'

'It's about you.'

'But why me?'

Turning the full force of her charm on me, she replies sweetly, 'because, sugar puff, there's only one you.'

As no one ever calls me sugar puff I suspect an ulterior motive.

'Is she always like this?' I ask the professor when we're alone together. 'What does she want?'

After a long pause he smiles his knowing smile.

'It might be publicity for your book.'

So when Elina calls the next day proposing we do an interview on tv I agree. And, as I'm old enough to be master of my fate and captain of my soul, I've no one but myself to blame for the consequences.

'I'm so excited,' she warbles on the phone. 'We're gonna have such fun.'

'Where's the tv studio?'

'You'll never find it, darling. I'll take you there myself. Come over to my place and stay the night.'

Protesting politely, I demur about staying over but she cuts in with, 'I've arranged for you to meet three gentlemen the evening before the interview. It's all settled. You wouldn't want to miss out on that, sugar puff.'

'What gentlemen are these?' I ask not unreasonably.

'Very important people, darling. Especially at the moment. They can barely spare the time.'

She phones again the following day. We discuss the interview and my new play.

'Darling, I'm so excited. I've got you a superb location. Don't be late. There'll be three men waiting for you.'

The professor drives me to her apartment on the Upper East Side.

'I'll leave after I've seen you safely there,' he offers.

Famous last words. Only later does it emerge that no one from the university has ever set foot inside.

Elina answers the door wearing a pink suit with nails and earrings to match. Raven curls cascade to her shoulders. The sound of male voices comes from within.

'At last the lady herself.' She smiles, partially blocking the doorway, so as to virtually exclude the professor. 'Come in,' she coos sweetly to me. 'There's three gentlemen waiting.'

It's an awkward moment. The professor hesitates, then smiles before declaring, 'I'll be off.'

I enter her domain. Purely for the sake of my work. As she closes the old fashioned solid door behind us I can't help feeling that the walls are thick enough to muffle sound. A panicky fear hits me. What if I become entombed? Like Senator Klein from Bronxville, who lay dead in his swish apartment for six weeks before anyone knew. I push the fear away.

'It's so . . . peaceful,' I exclaim. I was going to say quiet but, now that we're shut inside, peaceful has a more hopeful ring to it.

'We won't be disturbed.' She smiles, then playfully pushes me forward towards the room of male voices. 'But come along. Don't keep the gentlemen waiting.'

'Who are they? The film producers?' I ask.

'Sh!' She waggles a finger and girlishly leads the way.

Her sitting room is like an Aladdin's cave with a faded air of gentility: paintings of landscapes in gilt frames; lamps with silken shades on small tables; ornaments, photographs and books on every available surface. Crammed bookshelves line the walls. More books are piled high, higgledy piggledy, on the floor. Facing me are the men to whom the voices belong. All three of them: Bill Clinton, Ross Perrot and George Bush. On a miniature black and white tv that keeps flashing lights. The set is clearly on the blink. I swallow hard.

'These are the men?'

'Yes. Aren't they cute?'

Hardly. I sit on an aubergine sofa covered in printed corduroy.

'What a nice sofa cover,' I remark for want of something better to say. 'Is it Laura Ashley?'

'Yes, you clever thing,' she giggles.

'It reminds me of my agent's in London, only her Labrador kept jumping up on it.'

'No dogs allowed here.'

'Do you like animals?'

'Can't, can I? Not allowed.'

We sit side by side on the sofa facing a tv that's well past its sell-by date. Elina turns to me.

'Come on, have a drink. You've been rushed off your feet with the professor. Cheeky fellow. He keeps you all to himself.'

While she disappears to get drinks I take stock of my surroundings. The piles of books, balanced precariously, now strike me as being arranged less haphazardly than at first glance. On a coffee table there's a photograph of three boys with a girl, who could be Elina as a child. She has a mischievous smile and her dark hair is tied in a ponytail.

Elina's away quite a while. I want to turn down the tv but feel it would be impolite. On her return she explains she had to borrow a corkscrew from a neighbouring apartment, as she doesn't drink herself.

I apologise, 'Sorry. I wouldn't want you opening a bottle just for me.'

She laughs, 'Hush sugar puff. You're worth it.'

I sip a rather musty tasting wine while she gulps from a polystyrene beaker.

'Coke is as far as I go,' she says disarmingly and then disappears into her bedroom.

I hear the sound of murmuring - as if she's using the phone. From time to time I can hear sniffling and wonder if she's crying. Not wishing to interfere, I stay where I am facing away from the blinked out tv. I'm not sure for how long as I don't wear a watch and can't be bothered to search for the travel clock in my overnight bag.

· The three Presidential candidates are still blaring horribly when Elina emerges from the bedroom, looking a bit red and blotchy. Perhaps she was crying.

'Do you really want to watch them?' I ask, indicating the tv that's becoming a snowy blur. Apart from the faulty reception she's missed most of the debate by now.

'Darling, it's important, you know, for the country of America,' she purrs, 'and also, sugar puff, for the whole world.' Her eyes seem to have widened and are now dark blue pools of dancing light. She sighs, 'And people do need help. Like the less fortunate. You know. Those considered undesirables.' She pauses, then sniffs. With those red blotches around her nose she must have an allergy. 'I try to help where I can but I get a lot of grief at work.'

I nod, picturing her presiding at the juvenile court as well as squeezing in some tv acts of mercy. She gives a tight smile. 'I wanted you over here earlier but that pesky professor kept you from me, darling. I don't like people who do that.'

Her mood is slipping without warning into an aggrieved mode. I wonder if she's drunk but how could that be when she told me she only takes Coke and no liquor at all.

Suddenly she leaps up. 'This tv is a pest. Come on, we'll knock up my cousin.'

'Where's that?'

'Oh, just round the block.'

We leave the apartment and cross a lawn to a similar building which she enters with a key. We climb two flights. She takes the stairs at astonishing speed, bounding up like a gazelle in contrast to her stated weariness. I struggle to keep up.

'This is it,' she glances at me with glinting eyes, then knocks on a door marked 3 C., pauses briefly for an answer before shrieking, 'Police!'

At once four doors open.

'Go back girls, it's OK,' she soothes four Japanese ladies, who smile anxiously before retreating. Elina bangs again on her cousin's door. It opens a crack.

'Hi. Let us in. We need your tv. '

'No,' answers a small voice. The door clangs shut.

'Open up or I *will* call the police.'

The door opens and the owner of the small voice appears. She's tiny and wearing a man's overcoat, underneath which her bare feet protrude. She clutches the coat tightly to her. Her face is blotchy with red patches around the nose. She looks as if she's been crying. Poor thing. Same skin allergy as her cousin. It must be a family thing.

'You can't come in.'

But Elina now has her foot in the door. 'Why not pray?'

'I'm doing my warm-ups. '

'Poo-hoo! We all know about your warm-ups. Listen now. We need your telly. Mine won't work.'

'Get a new one.'

'On my salary?' Elina turns to me. 'She's a real joker. My cousin. Aren't you, Margaret?'

The overcoat falls open to reveal an emerald green tutu. With blotched cheeks and greasy hair she hardly looks the ballet type. More like Orphan Annie with those matchstick legs. Something weird's going on here.

'This is my friend.' Elina thrusts me forward. 'She's a film director. We're gonna make a film and guess who's gonna to be in it? Lil ole me. That makes me a film star. Can you imagine? Your cousin a film star! Now, that's something you didn't know.'

Margaret's brown eyes dart from Elina to me like she's watching a scary movie and doesn't know which monster is scarier.

'And my friend wants to see the election. She came over specially tonight to watch, and now she can't because it's gone on the blink.'

'What about the movie? I thought you said she came to make a movie.' Margaret's voice has a rasping edge to it, cutting and unexpectedly sharp.

'That's tomorrow, sweetie. Tonight she needs to relax with her feet up while we go over the lines.'

'What lines?'

'My part, Margaret. Why, whatever else would I mean?'

Elina gives a ringing girlish laugh that brings several people to their doors. As they retreat swiftly, Elina seizes her opportunity and pushes hard against the door but Margaret pushes back. Neither will give way. I smile politely.

'We mustn't disturb you,' I offer.

To my relief they stop. There is an awkward pause.

'Tell me about your movie then,' demands the bizarre figure standing there in a green tutu.

Elina's eyes gleam. 'I thought we'd film at dead of night. We'll shoot it downtown. An ideal location is the new funeral parlour where my friend here can perform her theatre piece about the wild seals. Celtic stuff. You'd kill for it.'

Margaret looks bewildered and is probably as confused as me. She protests mildly, 'But if it's a play why doesn't she do it in a proper theatre? '

'Margaret,' says Elina, as if reprimanding a stupid child, 'Rest–in–Peace is the newest and best funeral parlour in all Manhattan.'

'But what about Broadway? Wouldn't that be better - if as you say she's an actress?'

'Of course she's an actress. What d' you think I am? A goddamn liar?'

'No.'

'Then shaddup.'

Margaret's dark eyes fill with tears. I feel a wave of sympathy for her in her gross tutu, wrapped in a man's overcoat, shivering in the doorway.

'I think we should go,' I assert calmly.

'I'm cold,' cries Margaret.

'Then go inside for Godsake and wear some clothes. You look goddamn awful.'

Margaret smiles timidly at me. I smile back.

'Nice to meet you,' I say lamely.

'Gotta go now.'

Elina springs into action, yanking me with her down the steps and out back to her place, once more leaping with the speed of a gazelle while I vainly try to keep up. Where does she get her energy from?

'Hurry, sugar puff, we've work to do,' she exhorts when we reach her place.

I'm out of breath but Elina looks exhilarated. I sip wine while my hostess fills her polystyrene cup with more Coke from the kitchen.

'Is she all right?' I call out.

'Who?'

'Your cousin.'

'Oh, don't mind her. She gets narky and takes to doing workouts. Does nothing for her figure - as you can see.' Elina's dark head pops around the kitchen door. 'Her problem is she doesn't believe in herself.'

'And you do.'

'Gotta. Otherwise in this jungle you're swallowed whole.'

For a moment it looks like she's going to cry. Then she coughs and goes back into the kitchen.

Suddenly I feel tired. I long for my mattress on the maple floor in Eldridge St., the sight of Yonah Schimmel's and Needle Park, the noisy chatter of children on swings in the fenced in playground, the familiarity of Theater 80 and St. Mark's Place. All now part of my life in New York.

When Elina returns with more drinks she looks on the verge of tears.

'You know, sugar puff, I get grief not only on the bench but also in my private life,' She sighs, 'It can get very lonely sometimes.'

She gazes into her polystyrene mug.

I wait before asking quietly, 'Any men in your life?'

She sniffs. 'The last one was in a band- we had a number lined up - but then the poxy singer gets nabbed. You know.' After a pause she continues.

'When he comes to visit, my Pa's up on vacation. And the first thing he says is, 'When's the wedding?' She turns to me. 'Now, how can he have gotten that idea?' I shrug. Elina speaks softly, 'Then he's gone - you see he has to get money, you know - because of his – his need.' She pauses. 'Because of that he goes with men and women. You know.'

I nod understandingly. With Henry next door in Eldridge St. such things are now part of my life in this city.

In the morning after the interview I'll go straight back there. I'll get out at Bleecker St. and walk the rest of the way, pausing for coffee at the deli to steady my nerves. Oisín will be surprised to see me.

'Thought you were filming this morning,' he'll laugh, and after I tell him the news, he'll say something like, 'Drink this coffee and breathe in deeply on the veranda.'

That's the great thing about Oisín. A foot in both worlds - the aromatic world of coffee and the divine state of Yoga.

'So how's things?' I'll ask.

He'll grin and probably mutter, 'Nothing much.' Then, as I go to sit on the orange box on the roof, maybe he'll offer, 'It's OK. Henry is asleep. Busy night last night.'

And I'll nod understandingly and inhale the NYC air, watching Hank on a nearby roof doing his Tai Chi exercises. Poised in mid air. As if frozen. Oriental stillness. Peace. Freeze Frame. And we'll laugh and share another coffee before

Oisín departs for Theater 80, working behind the projector with reels of classics films in the real world.

But all that has to wait. Tonight I'm a guest at Elina's. A captive guest. Abruptly her sad mood changes to one of excitement.

'Sugar puff, we need a theme for the Halloween party. Something chic, glamorous – and outrageous.' She chuckles, 'Here's what I thought. Everyone comes dressed as themselves in the afterlife.' She pauses to gulp from her mug. 'After 9.p.m. only dead people are allowed into the funeral parlour floor of the building. So, we get in real early while the mourners are still there and have a few drinks on the 30th floor. Then -' she winks conspiratorially - 'as soon as the last mourner leaves, up we go to the 35th floor for the Halloween party of all time.' She chuckles, 'Just think of it. We parade as the spirits of ourselves in the afterlife while two floors below us - ' she breaks off convulsed with giggles, 'all the dead people are lying there in their caskets.'

While I try to imagine this bizarre scene, she winks. 'As for your play, they'll die for it.' When I protest that I'd prefer to perform in a theatre she won't have it. 'No, Rest–in–Peace is the ideal space for you,' she insists. 'All the right people will be there.' Then she laughs, 'Besides the setting is perfect. While you run over your lines, they'll put the finishing touches to their own costumes.'

She dismisses my further protestations with, 'Nonsense. This is the best audience you'll find. Especially at Halloween. In Manhattan.'

And in that moment my fate is sealed.

'I think I'll go to bed,' I yawn.

'You can lie on the sofa then,' she replies sweetly, 'seeing as you admired the corduroy cover so much.' As I draw the curtains she coos, 'No one will be peeping at you.'

I force myself to smile. 'It's just the light. I need dark to sleep.'

Sleep is impossible. Compared to Eldridge St. the place is very quiet. Too quiet. I lie awake listening to the sounds of Elina sniffling, her voice on the telephone, more sniffling. At one stage I think of asking if she's all right but obey a still small voice inside, telling me to mind my own business.

I spend the night tossing and turning until eventually it's 8.a.m by my travel clock. The last lap of my visit. Soon I'll be in the tv studio doing my interview. Immediately afterwards I'll head back to Eldridge St.

Elina appears at my side, looking grumpy. As I'm not a morning person this doesn't phase me.

'What time do we start filming?' I ask, hearing the sound of eggs, the great American breakfast, being cracked onto the pan.

Her voice coos at me from the kitchen, 'I've changed my mind about the interview.'

What? Is she for real? That interview is the only reason I've spent a sleepless night in her apartment.

'May I ask why?' I enquire coolly.

She laughs girlishly. 'It's my studio so I come and go as I please. Besides you've an appointment to see the Head of Film at NYU, and I won't stand in your way.'

So that's how she wants it. Suddenly everything falls into place. The sniffing and snuffling, the sudden mood swings. A knot of anger tightens in the pit of my stomach. If she regards me as just another loser then she's way off the mark.

Falsely bright, I quip, 'That's OK. I'll be off.'

She emerges from the kitchen.

'Don't bother to see me out,' I remark needlessly, grabbing my jacket from the closet and making for the door.

As Elina comes towards me I stand my ground. She no longer has power over me.

'Thanks for the hospitality,' I say with chilly politeness.

Turning to go, I half expect a hand to grab my shoulder and a voice to hiss ever so gently, 'Not so fast!' But she doesn't try to stop me. Our liaison is over. After all she's had her sport. Her cat and mouse game. First with her cousin. Then with me.

As I leave, a free woman at last, Elina's voice whispers in my ear, 'Don't forget who introduced you to the Head of Film at NYU.'

I manage a wry smile. 'Don't worry, I won't forget. Goodbye Elina.'

I bound down the stairs, onto the street. Outside, in the clear light of day, I find myself shaking from head to foot. From a sidewalk stand I buy two bananas, and devour them as I take three wrong turnings before reaching the subway.

When Elina calls me at Oisín's I ask him to pretend I'm out. Far easier that way.

Soon it's Halloween. Standing in the crowd outside the Tisch School for the Arts, I watch the parade, led by four models, the tallest, leggiest girls I've ever seen. These proudly stepping drag queens of Hope St. are the stars of the show. And, with such chic, glamorous and outrageous entertainment on offer, I've no need for Elina's fancy dress party, and can survive without her Rest–in–Peace type of publicity. Soon afterwards I leave for London where my play is performed.

I never see her again. Yet, even now, especially at Halloween, when children in fancy dress call to my door, I find myself thinking of Elina and wonder whether she's still playing trick-or-treat.

Nina & the Kestrel

Flying above the valley, scattered with cypress and olive trees, a kestrel glides past the mountainside monastery before swooping down to the lower slopes, covered with oak trees. The village of Lamira, a large spread of interspersed houses low on the Petalo mountainside, is literally covered with green. From the air the white farmhouse in Piso Lamira is only a speck. A church bell rings out on the hillside nearby. Far below the bird's flight, the riverbed, stretching along a crease in the base of the valley, lies hidden under verdant foliage. As the kestrel crosses the valley, morning sun catches the copper gleam of his wings, before spreading its light out along the headland, illuminating the white coastal houses of Hora, and making the sea shimmer like a jewel. You would hardly find a more fertile or lovelier island in the whole of Greece.

Nina's white farmhouse stands apart against a blue sky. On the balcony pots of every size and shape are bursting with flowers and plants; a cascade of colour and greenery trailing over the balcony wall down to the terraced garden cut into the mountainside. The house overlooks the valley and is surrounded by mountain on three sides. Below, on the shoreline between the mountains, lies Hora with its old town of narrow streets and tree lined squares, tall Venetian houses and handsome villas, several owned by Greek ship owners. High on the mountain directly across from Nina's home, stands the monastery, previously reached by a rugged mountain path. A new road, curling over the mountaintop from a village on the far side, makes the monk's famed hospitality and peaceful way of life more accessible to an increasing number of pilgrims from the outside world.

Once Nina found the four hundred year old farmhouse it was love at first sight. And now it feels like home. She often wonders whether he would have chosen to live here. Who knows? Right up to the end they kept searching for the perfect place, where he could paint away to his heart's content. During their long search some possibilities had proved tantalisingly elusive: a Georgian house in Ireland, the villa in Kifissia that he restored, a place in Dorset they bought, only to sell once it was renovated, and so on. However, like one of the restless birds he loved to paint, he preferred being on the move. For years the yellow Volkswagen van had served as a part time home with Jenny wren curling up in the back with her toys, singing herself to sleep. Later when the replacement van kept breaking down beyond repair he'd spend a month or two on Halki, the winter in Athens giving art classes, as well as teaching guitar and bouzouki. Somehow he had managed to find time to paint his birds of prey while Nina gave cookery classes, sharing the secrets of her *Cordon Bleu* skills with the wives of the Athenian diplomatic corps.

Now the fragrance of her lemon cake wafts out to the balcony from the cool, whitewashed kitchen with three-foot walls and a dairy fresh atmosphere. This is her domain where among pans and skillets she concocts ambrosial dishes. But Nina is not in her kitchen. Out in the terraced garden she waves at her Irish guests before gathering an armful of flageolets.

'All this beauty!' Mairéad sighs, 'Impossible to write.' She's seated under an apple tree, staring at a blank piece of paper.

Nina laughs, surveying her very own Hanging Gardens of Babylon. At first she required help with digging, hoeing, cultivating. Now, by rising early to tend her garden until forced indoors by heat, she can manage most of the work herself.

'Look!' Nina points to a rose bush. 'Only planted last year and it's sprouted two feet.'

'I don't know how you do it,' Mairéad declares, gazing at a profusion of lupins and marigolds near the vegetable patch.

'My apricots, plums, and strawberries just love this rich soil.'

'You can say that again!' Mairéad exclaims, inhaling the scent of jasmine. 'But don't you ever rest?'

'If I'm really stuck I get help,' Nina replies. 'There's usually someone, like Endri from Tirana, working on the island during the summer.'

'A powerful man with a scythe,' remarks Mairéad, regarding the recently cut grass on the lower terrace, where Nina's noisy chickens are pecking corn.

'Some racket!' chuckles Donal, who is sketching a view of Hora.

Mairéad laughs, 'Some eggs!'

'How many did you find yesterday?' asks Donal.

'Twenty two,' Nina replies, admiring her chickens.

Their egg yolks are so yellow that even the locals gasp. When she suspected the hens were laying in the bushes, she immediately enlisted Endri to carefully scythe the clumpy grass near the henhouse, that she had forgotten to lock at night. His strong muscular arms accomplished in minutes what would have taken her hours. Discovering eggs, he would shout and wave excitedly until Nina ran to the lower terrace, and gently transferred them from his careful grasp to her basket. She hands Donal a strawberry.

'Lunch will be soon.'

'When does Jenny arrive?' asks Mairéad.

'Depends on the Rafina ferry.'

'And taxi?' prompts Donal between mouthfuls of strawberry. Nina nods.

'Kostas will whizz her up in jig time.'

She can't wait to welcome her songbird daughter, who is training to be an opera singer in New York. Even as a baby whenever her father played or sang to her, Jenny had been fascinated by music. Later, exploring the Greek islands, they would both sing those same songs. He played bouzouki and she the baglama that he had made for her. As they drifted on the wine dark sea, she would beguile the gypsies by singing their Rembetiko songs. After music college in London and further studies in Italy, now she has chosen opera, and already her voice has the power to enthrall. Recalling how beautifully she sang to her father at the end, Nina sighs.

Afterwards, driven by desperate grief, Nina had sensed he wanted her to keep searching for the perfect place. And she did. After their years together she had a fair idea of suitable properties, and rejected several that were too large, too remote or sadly neglected. The fates being perverse, she had ended up, of course, with just such a place. Only this time she was absolutely convinced of its potential. The farmhouse, for all its neglect, held the promise of a real home for herself and Jenny wren. People were surprised by her determination and sceptical of the Southend fortune teller, who predicted that Nina would live in a white house surrounded by red flowers, even revealing the first two letters of the village she now calls home.

On the balcony she passes the large tabby snoozing on the best chair. Since he can eat for Europe she has hung bells on his collar as a warning to birds.

'Call if you need a hand,' Mairéad offers.

But Nina has disappeared through the French doors into the main room, which houses some of his paintings and musical instruments. It's wonderfully airy, with arched recesses half way up the high walls to the carved wooden ceiling. Despite her grief - or perhaps because of it - she had tackled the house renovations with gusto, even persuading a local craftsman to build a corner fireplace in the traditional island style. With its chimney shaped like a beehive and a mantelpiece of 300 yr old wood it looks like it belongs. And, Nina has further plans. Underneath this room are three large rooms awaiting redemption and outside, near the lemon trees where marigolds and daisies catch the midday sun, nasturtiums climb over outhouses, that will one day become an apartment and studio. Before she presses on with these plans she must somehow bring herself to sort out his papers, music and art work. She has brought the lot over from Athens but can't bear to throw anything away. His paintings of eagles and falcons look so lifelike that she wants to ruffle their feathers. The other night she even found herself dreaming of a bird, sleeping beside her on the pillow, the coppery feathers streaked with blue, red and brown. She felt comforted and had awoken with a feeling of peace.

Once in Halki, while fashioning a lute out of rosewood, he had confided how birds of prey always held a fascination for him. As a boy, climbing trees on summer evenings, he would hide for hours high among leafy branches, imitating the call of the eagle, convincing himself that his efforts would fool the very birds themselves. For, like Icarus, he was bursting with a passionate longing to fly. And, despite a lack of response from the eagles of England, he pursued his passion with twin talents of sight and sound, persisting with his birdcalls just like Wordsworth, who blew mimic hootings to the owl. At school he made sketches of the eagle's beaky nose, gimlet eye and mass of feathers filling the whole page. Gradually his stark drawings grew so lifelike that other children, producing pictures of nice little birds like robins, were frightened.

Birds of prey were not his only passion. For what he desired from life, life couldn't offer. Yet he tried, how he tried, yes, every time, to get to the heart of his passion, to pierce the core of what mattered, to satisfy his soul. Despite setbacks of time or place. Or people. It wasn't till later, much later, that he came to understand, like Icarus, how flying too near the sun brings not only rapture but also the melting fire of consummation. And by then it was too late. With a heart so full of passion, that no one life could satisfy, he was gone. Burnt out with longing and yearning, playing classical guitar and bouzouki, Irish and Greek folk music. Dancing the hasapico, making a lute or a baglama. Fixing houses, fixing engines. Or singing John Dowland's, *Oh, Mistress Mine,* as he accompanied himself on the lute. And, always painting; birds of prey, Greek papas, views of Crete or Halki or anything that caught his fancy. And it was easy to catch his fancy. For much appealed to him and he was far too appealing for his own good, attracting people to him like moths to a flame. They flickered about him, unable to satisfy his needs. In awe of his talent. As if they sensed his failure to grasp that being cursed by so much passion - though a torment - is the curse of genius.

She resolves to start arranging his things – something she must do if she is to put her own house in order. Perhaps when Jenny wren arrives – herself like a singing bird of fine plumage, whose heart piercing voice makes your breath catch in your throat.

Taking a vase of pink roses from the back kitchen, Nina climbs the corner stairs, painted white like the floor of the attic room. Places the vase on the dressing table. Arranges pillows on the white bed. Its canopy of gathered net, like a bridal veil, hangs over the brass bedstead and sides to fall softly to the floor. Adjusting a lace curtain on the window, she shuts the little door leading to the roof, where last year she plucked oranges from the tree overhead to make marmalade. Before turning to go she regards her handiwork. She has made Jenny's room so white, so fresh, so delicate, it resembles a haven of delight for a fairytale princess.

Nina returns to the kitchen to put the finishing touches to lunch. She has cooked Jenny's favourite. Spaghetti Bolognaise followed by lemon cake. She calls her guests inside.

'Open the wine, Donal, like the handy man you are.'

Looking at a tall painting of two Greek papas, Mairéad sighs,' I remember when he painted that.' She turns to Donal. 'Wasn't it on Crete? In that studio?' He nods.

Nina smiles as their talk turns again to the early times when they knew him in Dublin and Chania. That was before he met Nina and married her.

'I seem to remember the street was called after El Greco. Or was it?' Donal asks.

'You're right.' Nina replies. 'He was born there.'

Mairéad laughs, 'When we first heard the name Theotocopoulous it sounded like the Greek word for Chicken.' Nina chuckles as Mairéad adds,' I thought that El Greco was his real name.'

'No, you ninny. It means The Greek,' Donal corrects her.

Nina agrees. 'He signed his paintings in Greek characters, using his real name, Domenikos Theotocopoulos, sometimes followed by Kres, meaning Cretan.'

'See!' exclaims Donal.

'And don't you pair just know your art history!' Mairéad teases.

Nina gives her a look of mock severity. 'Set the table and behave,' she orders, handing her a blue and white tablecloth to match the Italian plates.

Hearing Donal and Mairéad recall the turpentine scented studio near the old Venetian harbour of Chania, Nina pictures him flinging wide the shutters, light flooding into the high ceilinged room as he sharpens pencils, cleans brushes, puts off mixing his paints while he gazes out at the Aegean, whose same waters now wrap her island in their embrace.

'He'd have loved it here,' Mairéad murmurs, looking through French doors up at the monastery, perched like a white dove on the mountain, then glancing downwards to the scattered trees, verdant valley. A biblical Arcadia.

'You bet he would,' adds Donal, refilling their glasses.

'I wonder,' muses Nina.

'No doubt about it,' insists Mairéad.

'I really must sort out his things,' Nina sighs.

'Perhaps when Jenny comes . . .?' Mairéad suggests, echoing Nina's thoughts.

Nina puts a CD into the player. With the high ceiling the acoustics are perfect for the voice of her songbird daughter. The house is filled with the sound. Donal and Mairéad listen intently and, when the CD finishes, burst into applause. Then, while they are still clapping, as if on cue, Jenny wren bursts through the door, to be covered in kisses and laughter.

Nina smiles proudly at her beautiful, dark eyed daughter. 'Welcome home, my love,' she comforts, stroking the black hair, curling down over her shoulders.

Returning the smile, Jenny looks around the room, regards her baglama hanging there on the wall. 'It's good to be home.'

After lunch Donal and Mairéad clear the table things into the kitchen. With a tinkle of bells the tabby lumbers in.

'Did you miss me, pusaki?' Jenny asks, taking him on her knee. He purrs loudly. Nina hugs her daughter once more, this time with a sigh.

'You must be tired.'

Jenny laughs, 'I could do with a rest.'

Nina smiles. They have lots to discuss. Later. After Jenny's siesta in her white dovecote.

'Lunch was great. As usual.'

Nina laughs, 'So I haven't lost my touch?'

'That'll be the day!' her daughter jokes and,

picking up the cat, his bells atinkle, goes out onto the balcony.

After a few minutes Nina follows her. The cat is again ensconced on the best chair. Jenny stands there, breathing in the air over the valley. A flutter of wings in the stillness makes them both look upwards to where a kestrel hangs poised in the air with quivering wings, demonstrating how no other hawk has so perfected the art of stationary flight.

'Look Mama!' Jenny whispers, pointing to the bird who gives a shrill 'kee–kee-kee' cry, then circles a few times before hovering over new ground.

'No wonder he's known as Windhover,' Nina murmurs and, remembering the bird in her dream, is filled with the same feeling of peace.

'It's like as if –,'

She breaks off to watch Jenny watching the kestrel, who glides forward to hover once more. She catches her eye. They smile as if sharing a secret.

Sweetie Pie

Tom didn't come home last night. I don't care. And let me tell you something for nothing. I don't mind if he never comes home again. And I mean that. You see it wasn't so much what he was doing. I mean to say we all have to make a living don't we? And it's hard making a living in New York. No it wasn't that, but how often. God, I sound like the priest in Confession.

'How often, my child?' Silence. 'How many times did you do it?'

I can hardly bring myself to tell anyone. When they asked me to write it all down, I thought of you and how I could always tell you things and you wouldn't laugh, like the others. So I'm writing it down. All of it. And when I've finished maybe they'll let me go. After all I did nothing. All the time I did nothing. In every sense of the word. I mean I'm not the one that has to go to Confession. He is. So I don't have to worry about a thing. I don't need to be afraid. After all I did nothing.

When I met Tom at the Pizza Place on First Avenue I thought he was the best thing that could ever happen to me. I loved the way he pushed his black curly hair out of his eyes and his slow lazy smile. I suppose I am a bit childish in a way. Maybe that's because my mother kept us under

107

lock and key. *We don't know who'd be looking for you, do we,?* she'd say. And then she'd smile. I suppose that was to make sure we wouldn't be afraid. She always smiled. Then she'd lock us in. Not in any cruel way mind. Just to keep us out of harm's way. Or so she said.

Maybe when I've written it all down exactly how it was they'll let me go, and then I'll cross the street to the Pizza Place on First Avenue. I'll buy a slice with pepperoni and get a can of diet Pepsi. I want to keep my figure nice. Men like you when you look nice. No one knows that more than me. I'll sit at a table near the door. Maybe when the wind blows the papers in through the café doorway I'll look up to see who has come in. It could be Tom. And maybe I'll tell him then. Maybe.

He was full of surprises, often coming home when I didn't expect him. It was the work he did I suppose. But I never asked. That was one of the ways he got around me. Surprise. I used to love the little surprises he gave me when we were together at the start.

One evening he came home with a fur coat. And it was for me. Now if that happened to my mother she'd throw a fit and think that the coat was stolen. But I knew better. I know what men are like. Not like my mother. She never had a clue. So when Tom came home and looked at me with that light in his eyes I knew there was something up. I mean a nice surprise. I shut my eyes as he asked me to and when he put the soft fur up to my neck I smiled and turned to kiss him.

'So who's My Sweetie Pie then?' he asked.

I didn't answer except with my eyes and he knew then I was his Sweetie Pie and not going to go off with another. I asked no questions. And we were happy. My mother always told me not to keep on asking people things because sometimes they don't know the answer and you only make them feel uneasy. So I never asked him anything. And that was just the way he liked it. He told me so often there could be no doubt about it. When he brought me home nice surprises I kissed him and he was happy. I'd have kissed him anyway but he seemed to think that I'd fall for him more than ever if he gave me things. Oh now, don't get me wrong. I love a fur coat as well as the next woman. Don't we all?

At the start I loved him bringing me things. Anything at all. Well that was at the start. I mean when a girl gets a fur coat as a surprise it's hard to give her a better surprise.

Then Tom got it wrong. Not that he could help it. It really wasn't his fault. You see he thought that just because I kissed him like I did when he brought me the coat that was my heart's desire. Dear God, if he only knew! I never liked the idea of animals being killed just so as you and me could go out all dolled up in their skins. But for the sake of peace I let on to him that I loved the coat. And in a way I did. Well at least I did the first time. And a couple of times after that. But when he kept on bringing me fur coats I knew what to expect. I mean a surprise is not a surprise if you know what it is.

That was when I made my first mistake. I told him. He wasn't pleased. He wasn't pleased at all. He stopped kissing me and looked at me with a hard look, the kind of look I'd seen him give the men on First Avenue when they tried to stop him for a light for their cigarette. At least I think that's what they wanted.

'So my Little Sweetie Pie doesn't want a nice surprise then? '

'No.' I bit my lip. 'I mean it's lovely Tom, really it is but -'

'But what?' He held me by the hair. I didn't move a muscle. 'Come on, tell dear old Tom what it is, honey.' He tugged my hair so that it hurt.

I began to cry. I didn't mean to. It just happened. You see men always like me and no one ever did that to me before. But when I tried to tell him I couldn't get the words out because I was sobbing. That made him angry. Tom doesn't like it if you cry. Most men don't. My mother always told me, *Cry yourself if you must but don't let on to a man that you're full of tears because that makes them feel uneasy.* Well I couldn't help it. You know what I'm like. A real softie. If I see a car crash on the telly I nearly pass out with the horror. It's like it was happening to me, and I cry. But only when I'm on my own. Once or twice I almost let Tom see me cry by mistake but managed to slip out to make tea and get him a drink before he saw the worst of my tears. One time a little child was dying on the telly and his mother couldn't save him. They were out in Africa or somewhere with a lot of strange animals and in danger. I couldn't get that little child out of my mind for a long while. Other people must be very brave all the time not to cry. My mother said, *Everyone cries sometimes but they never let on. It only makes people uneasy and gives them the idea that you are a softie.* Which I am. And I agreed with her but in my heart I wondered why you couldn't let the tears fall and why you had to keep them inside you or else rush off into a secret place to weep.

That day when he saw me crying Tom let go of my hair and ran out of the room. Then I let all the tears that were inside me flow like a waterfall. They made the fur coat all wet and looking like a cat that had washed itself. I put it on a hanger beside the other fur coats and turned the part that was wet with my tears towards the wall so he wouldn't notice.

Then I had an idea. As I looked at all the coats hanging there I thought to myself, This is crazy. I don't need them. So why keep them? I thought of all the people on First Avenue who'd give their eye teeth for one. So I picked out my favourite. It was the first one he gave me and if I tell the truth the only one that was a real surprise. All the other times I was letting on to him that I was thrilled when I wasn't.

I put my favourite to one side and put all the others into a plastic bag and crept down the stairs. He didn't hear me. But that didn't surprise me. Once he has a little drink he goes all quiet and dozes off. I forgot to say about his drinking. But then they said tell us everything even if it seems silly, and I did.

When I got to the front door the family upstairs was coming in. They're from India and even though it wasn't warm she was wearing a sari and sandals. Suddenly I felt sorry for her and reached into the bag.

'Here you are,' I said making it seem like an everyday thing.

When she saw the fur coat the eyes nearly popped out of her head. She went to take it but her husband stopped her. He smiled at me. A slow sort of a smile. His teeth were very white.

'You are very kind,' he said, 'but you will need that coat for yourself.'

'Oh no, 'I said quickly, and just to let him know it wasn't a joke I pulled out the other coats. 'Look, I have plenty.' And I smiled at him.

His wife looked uneasy and the children tugged at her sari.

'We will not take your kind offer but thank you.'

This time I saw his smile was quick and with a touch of pity in it.

'Suit yourself,' I replied, trying to sound as if it didn't matter but I felt hurt that they didn't want my surprise. It was then I realised that this was how hurt Tom must have felt when I didn't want all the lovely coats he kept bringing me as surprises.

So I screamed and kept on screaming until someone came. They still don't believe me when I tell them what happened so they told me to simply write it down. All of it. And I'm doing that as best I can.

Tom never came back. No one knows where he is. I keep telling them I did nothing but you believe me don't you? Maybe you think that as well as being a softie I'm gone a bit daft. You could be right. But you see Tom was the best thing that ever happened to me. I don't hold with all that Womens Lib stuff. People can get a job and be happy without a man if they like. I don't care. If that's their way. But it isn't mine. Men always like me and want me and that's nice. Maybe I could learn to be different. Maybe.

But then Tom could come back, you know. He could.

Holy Orders

His vocation came completely out of the blue. With the benefit of hindsight, you could say that the signs were there all along: the laying on of hands, missionary zeal, religious feasts. However, at the time we weren't aware of any devout tendencies on his part. Many who are called to Holy Orders cite a visit to Lourdes, a parish retreat or an authority figure, who influenced them in their formative years. However, he didn't take us into his confidence. And by the time the truth emerged it was too late.

We were amazed to discover that his vocation was the result of a subtle recruitment drive by the archdeacon's housekeeper. She was a delicate, bird like creature, whose campaign of tender patience combined with steely determination gradually enticed him to the religious life. Her means were of the utmost simplicity - and ingenious. To encourage potential postulants she began by offering food, drink and shelter in a convivial setting. As we were a family of healthy eaters, we soon noticed when he became uncharacteristically 'picky' at mealtimes, and soon understood why after hearing that she was supplying him with tempting snacks. We apologised profusely on his behalf, horrified that he was troubling such a pleasant and amiable soul, to whom 'all was conscience and tender heart.' We told our local version of Chaucer's Prioress that we'd move heaven and earth to prevent a repetition of such antics. However, she insisted that he was a most welcome visitor, her devotion intensifying when he began attending religious feasts at the archdeacon's. The latter was kept in blissful ignorance of these festivities. For whenever the holy man came down from his study to the dining room his housekeeper ensured that her protégés were confined to the cosy kitchen. There a cheery fire blazed away around the clock, ostensibly to heat water. Like the prelate, we were ignorant of the clandestine cavorting around the simmering cauldron of pleasure below stairs at the presbytery. Perhaps we should have been on the *qui vive*. But unprepared for the force of proselytizing, we failed to grasp that once a conversion takes hold it can be impossible to keep away from the Church.

Had we realised doubtless we wouldn't have accepted her offer 'to keep an eye on him' while we went away over Christmas. Leaving him to the strains of *Adeste Fideles* and tender loving care, we returned after a few days, and so did he - none the worse for wear. Seemingly, while away in a manger he'd made a lasting impression on his hostess, who found his friendly nature endearing. She enthused about his ability to socialize with permanent and casual residents, declaring he possessed a certain *je ne sais quoi* in matters of etiquette, unlike some B & B overnighters who tended to pounce on their companions when treats were produced. In contrast he displayed perfect manners at all times. It sounded almost too good to be true. Like he was destined for sainthood.

Like many of the sainted he had sprung from lowly beginnings. When he came to us through a notice in the *Evening Press* looking for a good home we'd welcomed him with open arms. He was a strong handsome fellow, very, very large with enormous feet and gleaming white socks. With his wide eyed expression and trusting nature he quickly became a favourite in our household.

Outdoors he established himself as a force to be reckoned with, a dominating black and white presence patrolling neighbourhood garden walls, his sheer girth making the walls impassable to others. From a vantage point on the roof of our garden shed he'd appear to be dozing – a favourite pastime – only to leap like a lion without warning on top of any unsuspecting intruder wandering through our back garden. In the house he exuded a sweet natured warmth – just as long as his needs were catered for. Blessed with a voracious appetite he could eat at any time of the day or night, and made up for not having a sweet tooth by sampling savouries between meals. Steering clear of vegetarian delights, he'd regularly devour hearty chunks of beef or a fine plate of salmon. If pushed he would eat tinned food but preferred the real thing. Slivers of pork or chicken, filets of mackerel or herring, nicely cooked turkey and ham, and so on.

After adopting him, we had rejoiced as he'd blossomed under our care and became one of the family. Yet, from the start, we had grasped the need to temper our welcome with respect for his independent spirit. We understood this but did the 'Prioress'? She'd often stop us in the street with a wistful air to bear witness to his happy nature and declare how much she missed him. With only five walls between our back garden and the presbytery, she fervently hoped that he'd resume his frequent visits. We failed to sense any hidden motive on her part and never suspected that he might become one of the chosen ones while she stressed that he was more than welcome to return at any stage in the future.

Such generosity in this dark world of ours isn't to be sneered at we told ourselves. And the following year we found ourselves seizing a golden opportunity. We'd mentioned that we were off to Australia for five whole weeks and would probably ask a member of the family to call and look after things while we were away. The 'Prioress' wouldn't hear of it and insisted on inviting her favourite visitor to stay. His previous sojourn proved how admirably the place suited him. Besides, he could be such a warm, tender companion, and surely we wouldn't deprive her of the solace of his company over the lonely Christmas period. We were touched by her generosity of spirit and sanctioned the visit before dashing out to buy plentiful supplies for the archdeacon's larder.

Confident that our pet would be safe and our parting purely temporary, we prepared to journey to the Antipodes with a light heart. We watched with a smile, as happily he sped up the hill towards the church to spend a longer holiday in sacred surroundings. On our return we thanked her profusely, anticipating a reunion and a resumption of the normal routine. However, to our astonishment we discovered that during our absence a conversion had taken place. While away in a manger over Christmas, he'd entered the novitiate. On Laetare Sunday he had taken final vows. We feared he was lost to us, snared by the enticements of bell, book and candle.

Our trip Down Under proved to be a turning point in his life. Before the call to Holy Orders his sybaritic habits had led us to believe that he'd continue enjoying life as a happy heathen, professing allegiance to no creed or divinity unless you consider the gods of Egypt where his ancestors worshipped the Sun. He took after them in royal fashion. In summer his idea of paradise was sunbathing for hours in a sheltered corner of the garden, eyes closed, face inscrutable. I often envied him. For what can be more languorously seductive than the sun's warming rays? And, if glaring heat prevailed, he knew when to call it a day, moving to a leafy spot or going indoors for a change of scene and tasty snack. A true hedonist, he lived for pleasure and, like most of us, once his needs were fulfilled, was a delightful companion.

Now he was suffering from an overdose of hedonism, with a penchant for sacred snacks proving his downfall. Fed royally in our absence, he'd gained so much weight as to be almost unrecognisable. We now suspected that, like Chaucer's Monk, 'a fat swan he loved best of any roast,' and tried to visualize his religious induction in that blessed kitchen. Wild imaginings seized us. We pictured him reclining like a sultan, toasting his paws by the fire, being fed titbits like a voluptuary at a Roman orgy. Previously he'd enjoyed hunting as a diversion from feasting and slumber. Now exercise seemed a forgotten art and his religious lifestyle didn't include the rigours of fasting and penance. While 'now certainly he was a fine prelate,' alas! it seemed that, like Chaucer's Monk, his feasting days were far from over.

Concerned for his health, we pleaded with the missionary. Could she please allow the convert to resume his normal routine *chez nous*? She was unmoved and continued to tempt him with tasty treats. As he became listless he'd lie for hours in a corner of the garden, a shadow of his former self -

except for his size. When he could no longer manoeuvre himself through his own special kitchen door, we explained the situation but the 'Prioress' wasn't impressed.

'Get a bigger door,' she urged.

The vet pronounced a severe case of over feeding and decided to keep the patient under lock and key for a few days. Letting him loose would only result in exposure to further bouts of missionary zeal. An emerging side effect of taking Holy Orders was a bounty of fleas – no doubt bequeathed by B & B visitors to the presbytery. It was virtually impossible to banish the infestation since we couldn't capture the patient to administer a dose. We gently and tactfully spelled out the situation. We were pleasant. We were firm. The vet's word was law. We - and we alone - were under orders to administer a strict diet which needed to be adhered to. Otherwise death might ensue. This was no lie for the vet had pronounced that unless the patient stuck to the prescribed regimen he might perish. Simple you'd think. But we had reckoned without the power of the church. Impervious to veiled threats the housekeeper ignored all instructions and continued with her mission. Like one of the sirens luring sailors to their watery doom, she pressed her charms with skilful grace and infinite guile. There was a delicacy about the whole operation that was baffling. With sinking feelings we asked ourselves,

What hold did we have over a religious zealot? And our hearts sank further when the convert vanished in late Advent.

A few days before Christmas a brightly coloured card arrived in our letter box. It was unstamped. The message read, *'Happy Christmas to you. I am at no. 64.'* The card was signed with his name, though we didn't recognise his writing. An enclosed photo showed him preening himself, resplendent amid the hollyhocks of the archdeacon's back garden. Evidently this glorious moment of surrender to the Church had been captured in high summer and kept for maximum impact. We didn't reply. To do so would be courting disaster.

In the middle of the cold war that followed the missionary suffered an accident to her leg, which meant that she was confined to quarters. Secretly we hoped the accident to be the miracle we'd prayed for. While immobility reigned maybe with luck we could pounce, carry off the trophy convert, and life would resume its normal routine. We called with flowers, which she appreciated. So far so good.

But once again we had reckoned without the persistence of religious zeal. The 'Prioress' stepped up her campaign with a series of phone calls, asking us to go shopping for special delicacies for our pet, then for other residents. Seemingly each postulant had its own preferred treat. While we agreed to the demands of a limping neighbour we could feel the pressure mounting as the phone calls intensified. Could we now please do a *special* favour and go shopping for the archdeacon's desserts? How could we refuse? He was a learned man and not given to prelate like feastings - unlike the visitors to his presbytery. We felt the least he deserved was decent grub. Several expeditions followed for the purchase of ecclesiastical puddings. This continued for some time. Only something major could halt the impasse.

We never wished the archdeacon any harm. I only hope the ecclesiastical puddings were not responsible when he passed away. We regretted a notable scholar and courteous neighbour, yet, shamefully I must confess that we almost sighed with relief. For with the learned man gone to his eternal reward surely his housekeeper would be moving on? And sure enough, soon afterwards the 'Prioress' departed to pastures new.

Our household began to return to normal. As the patient kept to his diet he started to look more like himself, his furry shape fitting comfortably through his own special kitchen door, that again worked like clockwork. As he began to thrive and regain his former glory, his eyes shone, his purring got louder and his socks gleamed whiter than white. He bounded upstairs with his previous vigour and enjoyed siestas on our various beds. Outdoors he took up a conqueror stance on the roof of the shed and held sway over any unwary invaders, hunting off interlopers who'd assumed squatters' rights during his absence.

We all lived happily together for a good long while until, alas! The Great Reaper called him to the purring part of heaven. When this tragedy happened we were in the west of Ireland, having left him with our daughter and her husband. On our return they broke the sad news, and brought us to his burial place - deep in Bushy Park, where he lies to this day. They'd laid him to rest in a thicket under hanging branches. After finding the perfect space, our daughter gently placed him under a carpet of leaves with his face peeping out. However, her country born husband, fearing foxes might be abroad at night, suggested a deeper grave covered by leaves. On a branch overhead is carved the first initial of his Christian name. His full initials are D. G., which also happen to signify, *Deo Gratias.*

I recently bumped into the housekeeper at the doctor's surgery. She was, as usual, the soul of grace and decorum. Things were working out for her in her new abode. It was a miracle, she said, to have found such a suitable place so soon after moving. Privately I wondered if perhaps her favourite convert had interceded on her behalf and even now, was on the way to beatification. Soon the talk turned, as I expected, to things feline and I had to confess that her prize visitor, like the archdeacon, had gone to his eternal reward. She was sad to hear of his demise.

In hindsight perhaps we should have been prepared for his call to the religious life. Maybe we even asked for it. After all, what else can you expect if you choose that particular Christening name? For, as any Latin scholar or ecclesiastic knows, *Domino* means: by, with or from the Lord.

Peace & Prosperity

On the shores of Clew Bay you can wander along the winding sea road to Carmoney, where sleek yachts are tied up at the pier. Yet, if you ask in the new clubhouse how the pier came about you'd be met by a blank stare. For now the talk is in foreign tongues as Helmut Braun and Pierre Labrousse exchange lobster recipes. And you'll only find a few, among those watching yachts sail out towards the islands, who remember when the talk all summer was of the new pier.

If you were a visitor you kept well out of it - or at any rate didn't take sides. All season long there was fierce division between those vehemently in favour and others who scoffed at the whole idea. This led to an impasse until eventually it was decided to elect a pier committee. This suggestion came from the writer Kenneth Wycherly, whose work, though rumoured to be noteworthy across the water, was unread by anyone in Carmoney. Since arriving a few years earlier to seek inspiration and, as he put it, explore the western seaboard, he had involved himself in local activities. Indeed, his gallant efforts were significant in helping to install the piped water, an enterprise requiring hand to hand local co-operation that was the talk of the county. He had the added distinction of not being an actual native and as such his opinions were respected. So it came to pass that he was elected committee chairman and Barney O'Meara from the county council declared his *aide de camp* with two local men Peadar Mc Ging and Jimmy Hoban bringing up the rear. A fifth committee member was required but the subject provoked such argument that it was temporarily shelved.

The first meeting of the pier committee was set for the Wednesday following Pilgrimage Sunday which meant that the rush of visitors climbing the Mountain would be starting to trickle away. It also gave the newly elected committee members time to plan.

As Jimmy trudged down O'Malley's hill with the milk can, he was thinking of Josie. Now there was someone who would be a useful woman on the committee. She was the one with the brains - and stubborn like the rest of the Hobans. His wellingtons squelched through quetch grass, cow turds and nettles. As he whistled a black and white mongrel came crashing through a clump of gorse, barking excitedly.

'Nearly home Shep! A sup of tay and buttermilk for me, Doggo for you, and a day's work done!'

He peered for a sign of smoke from Josie's small island but could see nothing. Clouds capped the Mountain, making it seem mysterious and remote. Like Josie. He hardly saw her these days. The accident that left her a widow woman had forced her to draw back into herself on her small island, where she now lived alone. She was fine, she said, with the peace of the ocean lapping the shore, and no one to cause her aggravation. Still, it wasn't natural to be so long without human companionship. He sighed, remembering how once upon a time they had been all in all to one another. Almost closer than brother and sister in the things that mattered. She was the leader and where she led he followed. But the accident had torn them apart. Here on the mainland he felt marooned - as if the strip of water separating them held the distance of a lifetime.

He looked at the wheeling gulls and then out towards the Atlantic, remembering the three yanks, all of them women, who asked to be shown the sights. Looking down from the top of O'Malley's hill with the whole of the County Mayo all around, they declared it the best view of any they'd seen - and they'd seen plenty.

'Bedad tis!' Jimmy had boasted with pride, 'Tis worth dying for,' and they agreed. They sent him postcards from all over. Later placing the cards on the clevvy over the fireplace, Jimmy knew that no matter how lovely those faraway places were his view from the top of O'Malley's hill would beat them all hollow.

'You can keep your San Francisco and your Rio de Janero. They're only trottin' after Clew Bay,'

he'd tell anyone who would listen at
Maguire's. 'Amn't I right now?' And whoever
was in Maguire's would agree and order two
more pints.

Maguire's, on the roadside half way between
Carrigmore town and Carmoney, was proposed
by Barney O'Meara as a convenient spot for
committee meetings. There was no mention of
drink. When Peadar said he wasn't pushed where
they met, Jimmy, just to best him, settled for
Maguire's. Then Wycherly offered the use of his
home - a gesture declared far too generous by his
aide de camp. Wycherly, however would not be
denied.

'But dear boy! You simply *must* all pop into
me. Oodles of space here at El Dorado,' he told
Barney. 'I'll ask Jason to make scones.'

Barney shuddered at the prospect. Better hop
into Maguire's for a drop before meetings. It
would put him in better humour.

Peadar leaned over his garden gate to look at
the sea with yachts and dinghies bobbing up and
down among the rowing boats. Yet he hardly
noticed them or the seabirds circling overhead. In
his mind's eye he could see lorries with loads of
cement, slowing down outside his gate, the
workers all mad for a chat - or refreshments. He
sighed with pleasure. Teashops, public houses
even - would open in Carmoney, helping to make
it a tourist's delight. He imagined a new clubhouse

where visitors, cut off by high tide, would be surrounded by comforting pints of Porter and home made sandwiches. He pulled on his pipe, seeing the new clubhouse walls rising up to separate his cottage from Jimmy Hoban's. With enough to go around for everyone surely old angers and resentments would melt away. Prosperity would bring peace. Peadar sucked on his pipe and nodded. The new pier would be an answer to prayer.

At El Dorado, Jason put a red and white gingham napkin into a rush basket and placed it on the pine dresser.

'They'll be here soon.' Wycherly's voice was querulous.

Probably his knee, thought Jason, opening the oven door.

'I say!' Wycherly peered over Jason's shoulder. 'Do keep some back for supper. Mmm, what an aroma!'

'Out of my way!'

Jason nimbly whisked a tray of scones from the Aga and put them to cool on a wire tray.

Throbbing along the winding road from Carrigmore to the sea, Barney O'Meara pressed his foot on the accelerator.

At home Jimmy left the milk in a cool corner and raked the embers of turf, still glowing in the fireplace. Shep barked until fed and then settled down beside the fire.

'You're a right lazy divil. Sleepin's all you're good for.'

Jimmy laughed and spat into the fire. He removed his boots and socks and stretched out his feet to the fire. Ah! That was better! He drank his tea and buttermilk. Time enough for El Dorado. Let them wait! And let them heed Jimmy Hoban - though mebbe twould be better to put in his spoke before Peadar tried to best him. He refilled the kettle. When it boiled he'd give the old feet a bit of a wash and put on clean socks.

In the kitchen of El Dorado Wycherly watched Jason turn out a new batch of scones.

'You're a wonder Jason.'

'Wonder is I'm still here with all I have to put up with.'

Wycherly laughed and limped over to the scones.

'Hah! Don't touch. Naughty!'

Jason gave a swipe with a tea towel at the thieving hand. But already the scone was smeared with butter.

'Mmm, delicious'

'That's it for now. Otherwise they'll be naught left for the company. They're for sharing, mind.'

Jason's tone held a note of mock severity as he hung his bistro apron behind the door. Wycherly licked the last of the butter from his lips and sighed.

'You off then?'

'Yes. Cows milked, chickens fed, scones baked. OK?'

As Wycherly watched him go down the path he thought how brisk and chipper he was. Jason always had time for a chat. Not like some people. You'd think in a place like this there'd be all the time in the world for the things that mattered. He eyed the scones and decided to steal one more before the devouring hordes arrived.

In Maguire's Barney O'Meara called, 'Same again.'

As it was too early for serious drinking the place was half empty.

'You're looking well Barney. Not a bother on you.'

Maguire's flabby chins quivered as he pushed a pint of stout across the hatch.

'Mud in your eye!'

Barney knocked back his glass of Paddy and reached for the pint.

'How's the pier coming on Barney?'

'Nearly all sewn up.'

'No problems from Wycherly then?'

Barney smiled. 'Sure wasn't he the mainspring behind the Piped Water?' and he laughed at his own joke.

'You could have your work cut out for you with that pair.'

'Jimmy Hoban and Peadar? Don't be daft!' Barney laughed. 'There'll be no trouble - not with plenty of prosperity round the corner.'

'Aye.' Maguire was polishing a whiskey tumbler. 'And mebbe then we'll get a bit of peace.'

His attention wandered to a cluster of tourists entering from the damp.

'Plenty more of those with the new pier.'

Barney winked, and Maguire winked back knowingly before checking the supply of cream for Gaelic coffees.

Jimmy set the basin of hot water before the fire and eased his feet into it. Josie used to wash his feet when he was a boy, splashing him with water, laughing and tickling his toes. How things had changed since! He sensed from remarks overheard at Maguire's that she blamed him for the accident even though he'd tried to explain about the freak wave, the faulty oarlocks and her husband losing his grip on the rope. After that she withdrew into her own silence. Too proud to ask for help - or forgive.

Since she became a widow woman she spent her winters knitting and when spring came would row over to the mainland to sell at the market. She'd scoffed at his plans for the piped water and refused his help with the cows. She'd manage all right she said. Besides there were the two lads - nephews of her dead husband - who'd help if she asked. But she wouldn't. She would do fine, she said.

He dried his feet and set to paring a troublesome corn on his heel. He sighed. Old Josie was stubborn all right but you couldn't get the beat of her for brains. If only there was a way to bridge the gap between them.

While Jimmy was paring his corns, Barney O'Meara was knocking back a few more quick ones. What he wouldn't give to leave this godforsaken hole for a cushy number in a Dublin office. He was ready for the Big Time, had been ready for a while now. He fingered the loose change in his pocket. All he needed were a few more votes. There was a price to everything.

At the sound of Swiss cowbells outside El Dorado, Wycherly limped into the hall.

'Here, let me take your things, Peadar.'

'Ah no trouble at all, Mr. Wycherly.'

Peadar was already putting his damp overcoat on the rush chair with the chintz cushion.

'Still damp?'

'Oh, soft enough.'

They went into the book-lined sitting room where a fire smouldered. A second tinkling of cowbells was followed by the sound of sniffling coming from the hall.

'Are ye there Mr. Wycherly?'

'In here Jimmy. Come on through. Peadar, I wonder would you . . . ?'

Peadar lumbered out to the hall where Jimmy
Hoban was removing his jacket. That mean divil
was up to something, Peadar thought, staring at
his back trying to guess what it was. Twasn't like
Jimmy to become a sturdy member of a committee
for nothing. You'd only to remember who was
first to get the piped water.

'Are ye long started?' Jimmy asked.

'Ah no. The important stuff has to wait till
we're all here.'

While they waited Wycherly offered tea and
scones, glancing out the window for a glimpse of
his *aide de camp.*

At last there was a loud tug at the cowbells, an
answering hail from Wycherly, and Barney O'
Meara, reeking of drink, swayed into the hall.

'God save all here! Are we all right for the
meeting? Hah Peadar! Jimmy!'

And he slapped both men on the back with a
vigour that startled them.

Wycherly passed scones and poured cups of
tea, knowing that the mysterious workings of a
committee needed time. Especially this pier
committee. He was a diligent student of such
arcane matters, and having started the whole
thing was prepared to wait now for suggestions
from the floor.

Jimmy was mindful of the waste of time taken
over the simplest matter. If only Josie was here!
She'd cut through the whole caboodle like a knife

through butter. And so it was that local gossip about the fisherman who sailed off up to Donegal and never came back yielded after a while to general discourse about the rising price of ham and Porter. This was followed by the inevitable summer whinge about favouritism from the parish priest in the matter of 'stations.' While Wycherly declined to comment on local church activities he protested vociferously about a steep rise in the price of pork. Eventually when it seemed as if the whole matter of the pier was forgotten they got down to business.

'More scones anyone?' Wycherly pleaded. The committee members shook their heads.

'How about a spot for the pier then?' Peadar asked.

Barney cleared his throat. With his teaspoon he traced a path on the teak coffee table. The others followed the spoon's journey with their eyes.

'But dear boy! A pier on that side of the island would attract no business at all. Too remote.'

Jimmy glanced at Barney before saying in an offhand way, 'Sure the road could keep on goin' along by Peadar's and down to the edge with the pier facing out to the leeside of Inisbeg.'

Barney moved the spoon sideways and frowned. 'Like that?'

'The very same.'

Peadar smiled to himself. The new pier on his doorstep! A procession of tourists passing his cottage - and all wanting refreshments.

'Splendid!' Wycherly clapped his hands. 'With the pier there', he pointed to the spot on the coffee table marked by Barney's spoon, 'the place will be full of tourists.'

Barney nodded, his eyes lighting up.

'They'll come in their hordes,' and he slapped Jimmy on the back. 'In their hordes!'

'What name will we give the pier?' Jimmy asked.

'How do you mean?'

'He means', said Wycherly, 'How make it a landmark for tourists?'

Barney was suddenly tired. Time he was back in Maguire's.

'Call it anything ye like. The main thing is, as from now -' he banged the table with his fist, causing the spoon to fly to the floor. 'The main thing is the dream has become a reality!'

All that remained on the coffee table to locate the pier was a small wet stain.

Jimmy was the last to leave. Wycherly waved to him from the door. Putting the scones into a Tupperware box, he sighed. Jason would be hurt.

As he walked home, Peadar could see every inch of the pier striding out confidently from the shore outside his gate to the sea. Twould become known as PEADAR'S PIER and why not with his own gate leading to it? He'd paint the small back room and take in tourists - in a small way to start with. He'd give them eggs, and he could always get milk from Jimmy Hoban. He laughed softly to himself. That mean divil had his uses.

In the pub Maguire was in a huddle with some of the locals telling a story.

'She came after me like a bullock!'

He wheezed with laughter. As he laughed, Maguire's neck shuddered and the rolls of fat reddened. Barney laughed loudly, mentally counting votes as he signalled for a drink.

Jimmy was staring out to sea. He could see the pier stretching from his cottage towards Josie's island like a beckoning finger. A kind of bridge between them. He could see the words HOBAN'S PIER painted on it, proclaiming to the world that here was a landmark for tourists. A sign of new life and prosperity. An answer to prayer. And Josie, reading the painted words, would know she was welcome home.

Now if you travel out along the winding sea road from the town of Carrigmore, you must first pass Peadar's cottage and after that Jimmy Hoban's until you come at last to Carmoney Pier. Although there's beer on tap in the new clubhouse, Peadar's no longer there to drink it. Josie is long gone. So is Jimmy Hoban. And Wycherly is rumoured to have left the area after some unpleasantness over a neighbour's septic tank. The nephews of Josie's dead husband are now grown men with children of their own. They graze cows and sheep on her island. As summertime visitors you can wave to them from the boat as you fish the bay for mackerel.

Yet some things never change. People continue to come to Carmoney for the glorious mysteries of the western seaboard, and to seek inspiration. And the rising cost of ham and Porter is still a prevailing topic of conversation in the shops and at The Schooner, Main St., where Gaston Mayeux has recently taken to serving an 'Early Bird Special' of *Guinness & Crubeen Tapenade.*

Snakes in
Cotton Hollow

They say that there are snakes in Cotton Hollow. You can sense them, hidden among the rocks and trees. That's according to Jan who lives near the Connecticut River. She's invited Conor and Sandy to spend Easter at her home in the woods close by Cotton Hollow. And this year they're taking Marsha, who's over visiting from home.

Driving up from Bronxville through towns and wooded countryside, the air is heavy - as if with thunder. Spring is late, bringing plenty of capricious weather; cold one day, humid the next. Conor has packed his golf and tennis things. Sandy shoved in raincoats. It can be mighty wet up there especially if the river is flooded. And if you're hiking through the woods and wander off you can easily get lost. It's the kind of place you go when you want to forget. The sounds of running water and wind in the trees fill the empty spaces of your mind. And, you can tell your secrets to the winding river. A river less mighty than the Mississippi, yet, in its own way, just as muddy and full of secrets.

Conor brings his gun. He wants to shoot rabbits but can as easily get the cats - provided Jan agrees. She doesn't. Too bad. He could've cleared the place of cats over the weekend. But no. Jan loves her cats. All five of them, and she's not going to have Easter ruined by his gun popping and banging all over the place.

'You can go out behind the barn,' she orders, 'and shoot cigarette cartons instead.'

So he does. But it's not the same as cats. He likes to get his hands on guns. If he finds something special at an auction sale he must have it. Their home is chock–a-block with weapons; Rifles, Dick Turpin pistols, sabres on the bedroom wall. Conor always tries to get the best.

Jan's house is warm and tasteful. A tribute to her skills as an interior designer. She insists they take her elegant boudoir, where everything blends rather than matching exactly. Here they'll sleep between French blue silk sheets.

'Marsha, I'm putting you in Debbie's room.'

Jan leads the way upstairs to her daughter's bedroom, a patriotic shrine of stars and stripes from the duvet cover to the desk with miniature flags, guarding a photo of Debbie's graduation.

'She's in Africa exploring wild things,' explains Jan, indicating shelves of anthropology books. 'I fancy trees myself,' she laughs, throwing wide the windows, 'and I don't believe in drapes hiding you from the great outdoors.'

Marsha laughs back, sensing that they'll get on. And glad she's spending Easter near the place where Wallace Stevens lived in a house called 'Asylum,' overlooking a dump. She feels a thrill at being so close to nature, recalling the poet's lines:

Last night we sat beside a pool of pink,
Clippered with lilies scudding the bright chromes,
Keen to the point of starlight, while a frog
Boomed from his very belly odious chords.

And at night, hearing frogs in the garden, rustle of branches at her window, Marsha opens her eyes in the dark, sensing the trees dancing outside in the woods. And feels even closer to nature.

While Sandy sleeps the sleep of the just, Conor can't get used to being without drapes. Waking at dawn, he's tormented by the sight of tangled branches twisting grotesquely. His eyelids sting with lack of sleep. Still, it's only for two nights. Then he'll be back in New York, secure in a darkened bedroom far from frogs and cats. Funny thing about the frogs. In England they lived right beside the haunt of the natterjack toad, so you'd think frogs wouldn't be much of a novelty. Yet, somehow, the frogs in Jan's garden make more of a racket than an army of natterjacks. Not that you can compare in any real sense. What with the natterjack being a rare species and all that.

Jan sleeps in Jonah's room. He's at college. Doing something scientific. Like his father. Only you don't speak of his father, who left one fine summer's evening. Just like that. Conor worries about Jan. With a heart as big as a house her kind nature could be taken advantage of. He hopes she'll soon find a nice man who'll look after her.

144

Ever since growing up together in Ireland he's watched out for her. Not that she asks for help, or ever did. Independent to a fault, she always manages to find time for what's important. Like her friends, whom she welcomes with open arms and French blue silk sheets at her New England home. It's a far cry from Cork city. But there you go. That's how it is sometimes.

When Marsha wakes in the star spangled bedroom the woods are all around, and a mewing Cleopatra is scratching outside. Opening the window to let the tabby drop onto her bed she hears the sound of a mockingbird in the distance. With the cat purring on her tummy she snuggles down to dip into one of Debbie's books about birds of prey. She keeps the bird pictures turned away from the cat who's soon dozing away.

After a while, lured by the smell of coffee, she gently extricates herself from Cleopatra's embrace and goes downstairs, leaving the cat spread-eagled on a fractured expanse of stars and stripes.

In the kitchen Jan is handing a plate of warm croissants to Sandy with one hand while pouring coffee with the other.

'They say there's snakes in Cotton Hollow,' she declares.

'Baloney!' Conor scoffs, holding out his cup. No one makes coffee like Jan.

'I know they're there,' she retorts.

He smiles wearily. 'Snakes! Come on Jan,

you're romancing. Ever see one?'

She replaces the coffee pot firmly. 'No, but the snakes are really there.'

'What you bet?' he challenges.'

She's unable to keep a straight face and bursts out laughing. Her gaiety is infectious and soon they're all chortling at the idea of snakes in Cotton Hollow.

Their laughter is interrupted by a knock at the front door.

'Mercy me!' Jan teases, peering out the window. 'If it isn't my gentleman caller!' She turns to Marsha with, 'Wait till you see my Eddie's nose, you'll die!'

And sure enough it's Eddie in his ice cream white Cadillac. Marsha finds him strikingly handsome with his proud Sicilian features; aquiline nose and brown, brown eyes that follow Jan with doglike devotion, making her glow.

'Anything you need while I'm doing my rounds?' he asks.

'I told them, Eddie, about the snakes in Cotton Hollow,' she replies, handing him a cup of coffee.

'Baby, there's no snakes up there,' he laughs. 'You're making the whole thing up.' He winks at Marsha. 'Don't believe that Jan, don't believe her.'

'You calling me a liar Eddie? You calling me a liar then?'

'I'm only calling you what you are, Jan.'

Conor and Sandy exchange glances and slide out to clear the garden pool. He worries if it's clogged by frogs and leaves. It takes a while. Soon they have blisters on their hands.

'Better us than Eddie,' remarks Conor, 'seeing as he's no chicken.'

Sandy, whose new yellow trousers have turned black and mucky, adds, 'But rich and handsome. Quite a catch.'

She breaks off, catching sight of Marsha who's now joined them. And, sitting there in the warm Easter sun, Marsha learns about Eddie.

'When he was a baby,' Sandy confides,' his mother walked into the Connecticut River and drowned herself. Just like that.' She sighs.' The other kids were taken in by friends but he was adopted by a pair of rich old folks.'

Conor butts in with, 'That was Eddie's luck. And how it is sometimes.'

Sandy nods. 'Being real old when they adopted him they were soon gone, leaving Eddie all their stuff.'

'And that's how he got the Cadillac,' Conor explains. 'Ice cream white, and long and cool.'

'He really loves that car,' she reminds him.

'Who wouldn't?' he chuckles, adding with a glance towards the kitchen 'And while they're still at it, I think I'll get my gun.'

Sandy settles inside the porch so as not to hear the bangs.

'Keep behind the barn,' shouts Jan from the kitchen.

Soon Conor is banging away happily

'Are they still bickering?' Sandy asks Marsha, who has a good view of the kitchen window.

'I think they're making up,' she replies, watching Eddie put his arm around Jan's shoulder.

'Good. Once they start they can go on for days.'

Sandy sighs, picking up a small black kitten and stroking it. 'It's always the same with a new man in her life.'

'Will it last?' asks Marsha,

'Does anything?' responds Sandy wryly.

That afternoon Eddie looks a treat, all flash and handsome behind the wheel of his snow white Cadillac with Jan beside him. Marsha bundles into the back with the others. They drive down to the river, stopping at the place of the first ferryboat crossing. It's near where Eddie's mother drowned herself. Only you don't speak of that. Not at Eastertime with the sun gleaming on the muddy banks. Sludge, thick and grey like the Mississippi.

As they drive on further Jan exclaims, 'See that land,' pointing to parched fields that stretch for miles.

'Call that land!' Sandy protests. 'It's all dried up.'

'Shame on you Jan!' Conor adds. 'Can't you remember home?'

'Sure, I can remember,' warbles Jan, her voice full of sweet mischief. 'That's why I know a good piece of land when I see it.'

Eddie chuckles and stops the car so they can all look long and hard at what Jan is pointing at. No one wants to hurt her feelings. It's tough enough raising a family alone without adding to her troubles. And if this is the best land for miles then she's stuck with it.

'Well, I guess we seen that land, honey,' Eddie remarks.

From the way his mouth puckers Marsha wonders if he's thinking about his mother jumping into the river that day when he was a baby. Of course he couldn't possibly remember any of it - only being told she'd done it. They drive on down by the farms, tobacco barns and newly occupied houses.

'They say it's all white trash in this area now,' Eddie offers. 'Not like the old times with farmers working the place and no one driving around in new jalopies with loud honkings to frighten the face off you.'

As Jan laughs, Marsha tries to imagine the old times when farmers lived there, working the place.

While Conor fidgets with his gun Sandy warns, 'Put that thing away before someone sees you.'

'That's the idea, he jokes. 'Once they get the message they'll go and leave the place in peace.'

Jan chortles, 'Oh, Conor, you sure know how to make a person laugh.'

And cry, thinks Sandy, remembering the cat he shot dead – by mistake - or so he said. The trouble with Conor is you never know whether he's joking or not. Sometimes he doesn't even know himself. And if he doesn't, how in hell can anyone else?

They drive on, passing Eddie's house and the house next door, that also belonged to him before he gave it to the town for an Arts Centre. From such tragic beginnings he's become generous to a fault with his inherited wealth. And attractive to women. As Jan can testify.

'His advanced years don't make him any less agile. *Au contraire!*' she'd recently confided to Sandy.

Back home she shows off her new dining room.

'Eddie,' she purrs, 'I'm wondering what colour to paint it. Any ideas?'

'Hows about white?' he suggests, interior design not being his strong point.

'Eddie,' she protests, 'but where's your imagination?'

He chuckles, 'You've got enough for the both of us.'

Jan laughs, 'Oh, you men!' and turns to Sandy with, 'Right now, I'm in two minds. Harlot-pink or menopausal-plum. What d'you think?'

Sandy, usually hot stuff on décor, seems to have trouble deciding so Marsha chips in with, 'Definitely harlot-pink.'

Her reply pleases Jan who bustles about, humming as she gets them all drinks.

'Marsha, we must take you to Cotton Hollow,' Eddie declares.

'As long as there's no snakes,' she laughs.

'We'll go tomorrow after lunch,' he promises.

'Be on time,' Jan orders. 'I'm making something special.'

On Easter morning Eddie drops by with a bunch of Easter lilies for Jan before gliding off again in his snow white Cadillac. The flowers remind Marsha of an Easter spent in a Greek farmhouse: mounds of lilies growing everywhere and not a glimpse of ocean; only the sight of cows' tails forever swishing and the sickly sweet smell of lilies.

While Jan prepares a sumptuous feast Marsha listens to the radio. To the others *Lake Woebegone* is now old hat but they indulge her, knowing she was a Garrison Keeler fan before he became fashionable. The house fills with delicious smells. Since Jan won't use the dining room until it boasts new furniture and walls of harlot-pink, Sandy lays the kitchen table with the best glasses and linen. Soon everything is ready, the ham decorated with cherries and apricots.

'Hey Conor,' Jan calls out, 'you can quit killing and come in. It's nearly time to eat.'

They gather around the table waiting for Eddie.

'He said he'd be here,' Jan pouts.

Conor and Sandy exchange worried glances.

'He'd want you to begin,' she offers.

It sounds like they're having a kind of memorial meal for Eddie who's gone to heaven. Jan dithers, gazes mournfully at the plates. Mouthwatering smells are tantalisingly close.

'Seems a shame to spoil the food,' Conor hints, looking pointedly at Sandy.

'No. Better not spoil the food,' she echoes, hoping that maybe after a glass or two of wine Jan will forget Eddie isn't there.

And that's what happens. They eat and drink and make jokes that aren't jokes at all but they don't care because they're all together in Jan's kitchen eating home baked ham and really enjoying themselves. All of them - except Eddie.

The door knocker takes them by surprise. They fall silent, joking suspended, while Jan goes to the hall and returns with Eddie, who looks pleased and sheepish at the same time.

'Where you been?' she demands.

'I'm sorry, honey. I had business in Bridgeport.'

'What business?'

'Jes business, honey. That's all.'

Eddie spreads his big hands in a wide Sicilian gesture of helplessness, and his brown, brown eyes smile with childlike innocence while Jan searches his face for the truth.

'Whoever heard of business on Easter Day? I never did. Eddie, whaddya take me for, eh?'

He grins sheepishly. 'Can I get to sit down Jan, baby?'

As he pulls out a chair she snaps, 'Take a look at this ham, Eddie. It's all cold now.'

'That's all right, honey. I'll just have some wine.' And he pours himself a glass.

'What! You're not going to touch the food I cooked specially for you?'

'It's all right, baby,' soothes Eddie, his voice surprisingly soft. 'I had something to eat over at Bridgeport.'

'There's nothing funny about you missing dinner, Eddie,' Jan scolds. 'How d'you know I wasn't thinking you were with a woman?'

He grins. 'But I was, baby. I went to see that woman – you know the one I told you of.'

And he smiles broadly, like everything's fine.

'What!' Jan explodes. 'You breeze in here, Eddie, and sit there drinking my wine, and you tell me all this time you're seeing another woman. You tell me this – here in my own kitchen.'

'I'll tell you outside if you prefer,' chuckles Eddie.

Sandy tries to change the subject but Jan keeps on hollering about business on Easter Day having a fishy sound to it – especially business that fills you up with so much food you can't touch a morsel of an Easter lunch prepared by someone you gave Easter lilies to. It gets too much for Conor, who leaves the table. Soon they hear his gun banging away outside.

'He'll kill something,' Jan shrieks, shooting daggers looks at Eddie.

'I'll go out to him,' placates Sandy, glad to have a chance to leave the table where Jan's eyes are pricking holes in Eddie's gentle helpless face. Marsha would go too but he stops her.

'Naw, don't you go.' He eyes the remains of the feast. 'Look Jan, why don't we bring this delicious food over to Cotton Hollow and show Marsha there's no snakes?'

'But there are snakes,' Jan hisses, her eyes bright with battle.

'Then prove it,' he challenges.

While they're still arguing Marsha slips outside to tell the others about the trip to Cotton Hollow.

'Great!' Conor exults. 'I can get some snakes.'

They all pack into the Cadillac and drive a short way through the woods.

Coming down into Cotton Hollow, Conor springs ahead with the picnic basket. They follow to the place he has chosen. A stream gurgles over stones with trees reaching far above them on the slope. A perfect spot. They gather round the red and white gingham tablecloth spread with the picnic. A perfect scene. Marsha gets her camera. While she's still clicking they hear a cry. A faint, frightened sound. Marsha wonders if it's an animal but manages to keep her finger on the camera button. She has spoiled some of her best shots by getting excited at the wrong moment.

'What's that?' cries Sandy.

'Probably someone bitten by a snake,' jokes Conor, and rushes off with his gun through the trees.

'Should we go and see?' offers Marsha. 'It might be hurt -' she trails off, seeing the others tucking into apple pie.

'Live and let live,' chuckles Eddie, who's smoking too near the food for Jan's liking.

In the still air a shot rings out followed by a rustle in the trees. Conor appears looking pleased.

'Did you get the snake?' asks Jan, her eyes wide with alarm.

'More than likely,' he laughs, laying down his gun near the tablecloth.

'Put that thing away,' orders Sandy.' You're making me nervous.'

'Can't be too careful where snakes are concerned,' he counters, placing the gun out of sight behind a rock.

'You're so right,' Jan replies, shooting a look of venom towards Eddie, who's gazing off into the woods.

'Now, how about some food?' demands Conor. 'I'm famished.'

'That fresh air sure makes you peckish,' Jan agrees, cutting another slice of pie. No one mentions the sound. As Eddie goes to speak she interrupts with, 'Hush now, Eddie, and eat up.'

By the time they leave for Bronxville the moon is rising over the wooded countryside. Conor can't wait for his own bed with darkened windows, closed tight against the night. Sandy wonders how she'll tell him that they're history, and she's off to Europe to fresh fields and pastures new. Marsha, full of a lovely Easter break, waves out the back window at Jan, predicting a bright future for her – with or without Eddie. And imagines, deep in Cotton Hollow, a sinuous form glistening in the moonlight.

ISBN 142514977-4